MW00993377

Bob Morgan's bedtime stories are now featured in the following newspapers:

The Palatka Daily News, Palatka, Florida
The Cordele Dispatch, Cordele, Georgia
The Creekline, Jacksonville, Florida
The Coffee County News, Douglas, Georgia

Publishers of these newspapers have been gratified by both reader response and sponsorship for Bob's stories.

Syndication efforts are now underway, and we may soon look forward to seeing Bob Morgan's wonderful bedtime stories in newspapers throughout America, and the world.

We are privileged to bring you this first book of Bob's fifty best stories…a second book is already being planned.

Please join us in the growing audience of 'Bob-Fans', and revel in the simple delights of tales well told.

The Publishers
Pelican Press

Bob-Tales

By Bob Morgan

Illustrations by Amy Banton

Pelican Press

Cover design and illustrations
By Amy Banton

Artwork for Bob-Tales
©2003 Amy Banton

Printed in the United States of America

ISBN: 1-888562-06-4

Pelican Press
P.O. Box 4522
St. Augustine, FL 32085-4522
904-377-5239
pelican@se.rr.com
www.booksonnet.com

For quantity purchases, contact the publisher,
Ingram, or Baker and Taylor.

ACKNOWLEDGEMENTS

First, I would like to thank our Creator, for He is the one who gave us this beautiful world in which we live, and about which I love to write.

I owe all the rest to my loving wife Sandra, known to one and all as "Sam," and to our entire family, for the words of encouragement everyone has given me over the years. Without family, we would all be nothing. My friends seem to fit into this category as well . . . family, that is.

A personal thank you note to Rusty Starr, the publisher of The Palatka Daily News, in Palatka, Florida, for his willingness to publish my first story. He has been brave enough to encourage me through all of this, and believe it or not, he is still printing my stories. Thanks, Rusty!

A final word of thanks to both Mr. Preston Hardin, a school teacher and a good friend, who I have admired all my life, and to Ms. Karen Jones, a high school teacher, and a heroine of mine. These two poor souls undertook the thankless and daunting task of trying to keep my spelling, grammar, and punctuation within the bounds of reason. Thanks to you both! Any errors which may remain are all on my account.

Bob Morgan

BOBTALES CONTENTS

BOBTALES CONTENTS (Continued)

A LITTLE EGG

Once, there was a little egg lying on the ground in a farmer's pasture.

Since the little egg was all by himself, he didn't know who he was. His parents had already left him to grow up all alone, as a lot of birds and animals do.

I wonder who I am and what my name is, thought the little egg.

He looked around, and saw a bird perching in the treetop.

I hope I am not a bird. Look at that bird. All he is doing is eating those hard seeds from the bushes, and they don't look very tasty. I sure hope that I am not a bird, thought the little egg.

Then he saw a beautiful horse.

I hope I am a horse. He is eating that tender green grass, and the farmer brushes his coat every day, and makes him look so nice. But horses don't come from eggs, so who am I? thought the little egg.

Then he saw a cow.

I hope I am a cow. Look at the beautiful eyes she has. And cows get to stand in the shade all day, and chew their cud. They also make beautiful 'moosic' with their deep voices. But cows don't come from eggs, so I can't be a cow. I sure, sure hope that I am not a bird, **thought the little egg.**

He saw a pig playing in the mud.

I hope I am a pig. Look at all the fun he is having playing in that mud. I hope I am a pig. But pigs don't come from eggs, so who am I? **thought the little egg.**

Then it happened!

The little egg's shell began to crack open.

What is happening to me? **the little egg wondered. He broke all the way open, and came out of the eggshell. He could walk.** *What am I?* **He walked very well so he went down to the farmers barn. He found a mirror sitting next to a big haystack, and he looked at himself for the first time.**

"Oh No" he shouted, "I am a bird!"

The little bird grew up eating those hard seeds, which to his surprise tasted pretty good.

Then he realized that he could fly.

"Wow! Look at all of the beautiful things that I can see from way up here," he said. He could see things that all of the animals who were stuck on the ground would never see.

The horse saw him flying, way up there in the sky.
The cow saw him flying safely, anywhere he wanted to go.
The pig saw him, and wished that he could fly, too.

They all wished that they could be a beautiful, free bird, just like that big American Eagle flying up there. Now, close your eyes and picture yourself soaring high up in the sky, imagine yourself to be a spectacular, American Bald Eagle.

Good night.

LEWIS, THE LIGHTNING BUG

Lewis was a lightning bug, but he was no ordinary lightning bug. When he lit up, he really lit up. He was so bright that you could him see for miles and miles, even on a very dark night. All of the other lightning bugs would not play with him, because he was so different. But Lewis was a very good and sensitive boy-bug, and he was deeply saddened when the other kid-bugs avoided him.

In the same yard where Lewis lived, there was the house that Johnny lived in. And poor little Johnny had a problem. He was always afraid to go to sleep at night, because he thought that he heard noises under his bed. It was always dark underneath his bed, and Johnny was afraid to look under there to see what might be lurking beneath his bed. Johnny's mother and father would always look under the bed for him, and tell him that it was all right, that there was nothing under there to be afraid of. But once they shut his bedroom door, Johnny would hear those same noises again. It would frighten him so much, that he just could not go to sleep. Actually, there were no noises, Johnny's imagination just made him think there were.

One day, just as it began to get dark, Johnny was

playing in his yard, when he saw Lewis the lightning bug light up. Boy, was that Lewis bright. Johnny crept over to Lewis, and noticed the sad look on his face.

"Why are you so sad?" Johnny asked Lewis.

"No one likes me, because I am too bright," Lewis said.

"Well, I like you just because you are so bright and so different." Johnny said.

So, Lewis and Johnny became good friends that day. They played and played until Johnny had to go into the house to get ready for bed. Then Lewis just flew on up to Johnny's bedroom window to stay there for the night, in order to remain close to his new friend. He saw Johnny go to bed, and told him good night. Then Lewis went to sleep. But something woke him up. It was Johnny crying, because he was afraid to go to sleep. Once again, Johnny just knew that there was something under his bed.

Lewis tapped on the window, and Johnny let Lewis fly in.

"What is wrong, Johnny?" Lewis asked. "I noticed that you were crying."

"Every night when I try to go to sleep, I hear noises under my bed, and I am scared," Johnny said.

"Let me take a look," Lewis said. He flew under the

bed, and turned on his lightning bug light, and showed Johnny that there was nothing under the bed after all. That light really lit the bedroom up!

JOHNNY AND LEWIS LIGHTNING BUG LOOK UNDER JOHNNY'S BED

"I'll tell you what" Lewis said, "I'll sleep under your bed tonight, and every time you think you hear a noise, just poke me and I will light up so that you can see for yourself that there is nothing under the bed."

"Will you, please?" Johnny asked Lewis. "If you do that, I will finally be able to sleep all night."

So Lewis and Johnny went to sleep, and do you know what? They both slept all night. They were both happy, and couldn't wait until the next day, so they could both play with their newest best friend.

Time for bed. Lights out. You too, Lewis!

Good night.

THE UGLY BIRDHOUSE

Now, most bedtime stories begin with "Once upon a time," but not this one. This one happened just a few weeks ago. Here is the story, and this is what really happened.

A family of robins was heading south for the winter. As you know, a lot of birds do this. They like to spend their summers in the north, where it is cool, and they like to spend their winters in the south, where it is warm.

There was a mother robin, and her name was Etta. Then there was the father robin, and his name was Mike. And, of course, there was the little baby robin. His name was Daniel.

They spent almost the entire day flying. Now it was getting dark, and they had to find a safe place to spend the night. They looked and looked, and couldn't find a good place to stay. Finally, they found a birdhouse which was old, and it didn't look very sturdy. It was a very old birdhouse needing paint, and it just looked terrible.

Mike said to Etta, "I know it isn't very pretty, but we must stay here. It's getting very late, and we won't find anything else tonight."

Etta thought and thought. "You are right Mike, we'll just have to make do the best we can with it." Mike went out to find some food for his family, while Etta looked around at that ugly, old birdhouse. She said, "I think I may be able to help fix up this little old house."

Etta flew out into the countryside and found a ripe red berry. She carried it back to the birdhouse. Then, Etta took the juice from that red berry, and she used it to paint the perch porch. She flew back into the woods again, and found a plump blackberry, which she used to paint the outside walls of the old birdhouse. Young Daniel watched in amazement as his mother began to work on that old bird house.

Just then, all the other birds came over to see what she was doing with those berries. They laughed at Etta.

"You will never make that house look pretty," they all peeped. Laughing, the other birds flew away to their more beautiful homes. It really hurt Daniel's feelings, seeing them all laugh at his mother. Poor Daniel. But mother Etta knew better.

"Daniel," she chirped, "you are very tired, so close your eyes and get some sleep. When you wake up, you will see what a difference some loving care can make."

Etta knew that she could make that house pretty. She found some green berries, and painted the steps to the house a bright green. Then she found some blueberries, and oh, how pretty they were. She painted the rest of the house with that pretty, blue juice.

Mike finally returned with some food for his family, and saw what Etta had done to the house. He could hardly believe how pretty Etta had made that ugly old house. When Daniel woke up, he thought it was the most beautiful house that he had ever seen.

The other birds came by when the bird-word got around, about what Etta had done to that old, rundown house.

It is beautiful! they all thought.

"I want it!" a bluejay said.

"No, I want it!" peeped the redbird.

"NO, I want it!" screeched the blackbird.

Well, you surely know that Etta and her family kept that old birdhouse for themselves. After everyone else had laughed at it, Etta had turned it into a beautiful home. Mike and baby Daniel were sure proud of what momma Etta had done. Momma Etta put her family's name on that house, so that next year when they flew through here again, they would have that beautiful house waiting just for them.

Now, most bedtime stories end with "and they lived happily ever after." Well, it only seems right that this one should end that way, too.

And they lived happily ever after!

Now close your eyes, and try to picture what that colorful birdhouse looked like, after Etta got through making it beautiful... can you picture it in your mind?

Good night.

FIXING UP THE UGLY BIRDHOUSE

THE SHOEMAKER
AND THE CENTIPEDE

Once there was an old Grandpa who made shoes. He was a kindly old man, and everyone who lived on his street loved him.

He was thoughtful in every way. The old man even gave away the shoes that he made to some people who didn't have a lot of money. Why, one time he even made a special pair of shoes for a little girl who wanted to learn how to tap dance.

But the kindly old Grandpa wasn't making enough money to keep his shop open. He didn't know what he was going to do. But, he was too kindhearted to ask the many needy people to pay for the shoes that he made for them. If a little boy wanted a bicycle, but needed shoes, the little old Grandpa would tell him to buy the bicycle, then he would give the little boy the shoes.

What a good old Grandpa!

Little Cindy Centipede lived just up the street from the shoemaker. Now Cindy had a real problem. Her feet would always get very cold in the wintertime, and they would get hot in the summertime. The street that Cindy lived on was paved and boy, was it uncomfortable.

One day Cindy walked by the shoemaker's shop, and saw a very sad look on his face. Cindy had always seen him smiling, but never wearing a frown.

"What is the matter?" she asked.

"I am going to have to close my shop, since I am not making enough money to keep it open," he said slowly.

"You know what?" Cindy said. "What you need is to let everyone know about these beautiful shoes you have made. The only people who know about them is the people that live on this street."

"Why yes, that would work," he said. "But how will I be able to let everyone know?"

Cindy thought and thought.

"I know," she said. "I know the answer!"

Cindy went all over the store picking up pairs of shoes. She picked up fifty pairs of shoes, and put them all on, one pair behind the other (Did you know that centipedes have one hundred feet?).

Then Cindy walked all over town, and told everyone she saw where they could buy those pretty shoes. And with Cindy wearing them, everyone thought that they were very special. And, of course they were.

The little old Grandpa sold every shoe that he could make after that. He never had to worry about having to close his shop again.

And as for Cindy, her feet never got too hot or too cold again. If you ever get to visit her town, look for a centipede with fifty different pairs of shoes on. It'll be Cindy.

Cindy and the kindly, old shoemaker say, "Good night".

THE CENTIPEDE AND THE SHOEMAKER

LEBAU, THE SQUIRREL

Lebau was a squirrel who lived deep in the woods with his little brother, Norman.

Now, Lebau wasn't like most squirrels, for you see, he was afraid to climb trees. He was really frightened of high places, which can work to your disadvantage if you happen to be born a squirrel.

Lebau's little brother, Norman, however, wasn't afraid of anything. Norman would scurry up and down trees without ever being afraid. He would run across meadows, and jump over the biggest holes you have ever seen. Norman once even climbed a very high flagpole, all by himself!

Lebau would just sit on the ground and watch Norman having lots of fun, and he would wish so badly that he could do the same things that Norman could do. But Lebau was too afraid.

All squirrels love nuts, especially Lebau. But he always had to gather the nuts that had fallen to the ground. Those fallen nuts were always too ripe, or they were the ones that the other squirrels didn't want and had tossed to the ground. Poor Lebau!

Winter was coming soon, and all the squirrels had to store their food, for that cold, snowy time, when nuts were hard to find. They had to have enough food stored to last until Spring, when the trees would start growing nuts again.

Lebau didn't have any nuts stored...he could only find enough on the ground to keep himself from being hungry now.

One late Fall day, Lebau was looking for nuts on the ground, when he looked up at the biggest tree he had ever seen. It seemed to reach up, and up, forever. And was it ever loaded with his favorite nuts.

Oh, no! Lebau thought to himself, *How am I going to get those nuts down?* He thought about throwing sticks at the nuts, but he couldn't throw a stick that high.

Then, along came brother Norman. "I'll get those nuts for you, for you are my brother, and I love you, and I am not afraid to climb."

"Oh, thank you, Norman" said Lebau, "I'll be happy to share them with you."

Norman climbed and climbed, until Lebau could no longer see him.

Then Lebau heard the sound of a branch cracking. "Help! Help!" he heard Norman cry. "I'm on the end of a branch, and it's breaking. I'm afraid to move."

"Be still," Lebau shouted, "I'll call for help."

Then he remembered that no one knew about this tree. *They'll never find us*, he thought.

Lebau heard the branch crack some more. "Hurry! Hurry!" Norman shouted. "It's going to break off soon."

Without thinking about being scared, Lebau scampered up that big old tree. He got as close to Norman as he could. Then he stuck out his paw for Norman to grab. And just as Norman grabbed Lebau's paw tightly, the branch went tumbling to the ground.

Norman gave his big brother a huge hug and said, "Now I can gather these nuts for you."

But Lebau looked around, and after he saw how beautiful the world was from way up there, he said, "Thank you, but I'll gather my own nuts now. There's nothing to be afraid of up here, and from now on I'll never be afraid to try something new again."

Lebau knew that he would never again go hungry, and that he would always be able to find nuts enough to store for the winter.

So, you could truly say that those two brothers really helped each other that day, don't you think?

Lebau and Norman are getting ready to go to bed now, up in the top of that big, old tree, but they said to tell you...

Good night.

HOMA JR., THE CONDOR

Homa Jr. was a condor who lived on a high cliff in the mountains far, far away.

Now Homa Jr. was a really, really big bird. All of the other birds thought Homa Jr. wasn't very smart, because he was so big.

They would tease him all the time. They would ask him, "What is two plus two?"

Homa Jr. would answer, "Five." He knew that the right answer was "four," but that was his way of teasing them back.

The treetops would be full of birds singing their sweet melodies. You could hear them from far away. Their songs were so pleasant to hear. Even the trees seemed to love the music of the birds, and would sway back and forth with the help of the breeze, as they were listening to the sweet songs.

Homa Jr. would fly up to the treetops to join in the singing, but when he landed on a branch it would break, since he was so big.

Even when he perched on a big rock and tried to sing, it was awful. His voice was so deep that it sounded like a locomotive with something missing. He couldn't sing even low notes, and high notes were simply out of the question.

Some days the other birds would play birdie games. One of their favorites was to fly between small trees, zigzagging their way through them all, and howling with laughter as they missed each tree by inches.

Whenever Homa Jr. tried to play this game with them, why, he was so big that he broke the tree branches, and sometimes even broke the trees themselves. And, of course, the rest of the birds got a big laugh watching Homa Jr. making (what they felt) was a fool of himself.

Homa Jr. was just too big to play these games.

He couldn't hold a twig to build a nest like most birds do, because his talons were so big. He had to live in a cave on the mountaintop. But the cave was a large one, so Homa Jr. felt very comfortable there. He had actually made a nice home, with everything that he needed right there.

One day the other birds wanted to play hide and seek, but Homa Jr. was so big that he couldn't find a place to hide. So he decided to just go home. *They will never play with me,* he thought. Poor Homa Jr.!

Months and months passed with Homa Jr. having no

one to play with. Then, one morning, all the birds and animals smelled something that they all dreaded to smell. It was smoke from a forest fire! The fire spread quickly and came closer and closer.

"What are we going to do?" asked all of the birds and animals.

The animals said, "We can't fly like birds, so we are scared."

The little birds said, "We can't fly high enough to get above the fire and smoke, so we are scared, too."

Homa Jr. was sitting high up on the mountainside, and he could see everything. He saw the fire and smoke.

Now, Homa Jr. was used to flying high. He could even fly as high as the clouds if he wanted to. He thought about all of the little birds and animals down there in all of that danger, and knew that he had to do something to help them. So he took off flying straight down into the forest where his friends were.

"Quickly," he shouted, "As many of you as possible jump on my back, and hold on. I can fly you out of here!"

Trip after trip, Homa Jr. carried the birds and animals to a safe place across a river that ran down from the mountains. He didn't stop until everyone was safe!

"Thank goodness Homa Jr. is so big and strong," everyone said.

"I'm glad he was here," said the armadillo.

"Me, too," said the opossum.

"Me, too," said the raccoon.

"Me, too," echoed all of the other birds and animals.

At the end of the day, Homa Jr. flew back to his home feeling tired, but also feeling pretty good about himself. He was glad that he could help his friends. And you know what? All of the birds and animals were feeling pretty good about Homa Jr., too.

The next day, everyone decided to always play games that Homa Jr. could play, because they wanted their best friend to play with them from then on.

Good night.

Bob Morgan

HOMA JR., THE REALLY, REALLY BIG BIRD

TWO SEEDS

Deep in the forest, a long time ago, two seeds fell to the ground. One was an acorn, and one was a pine.

Rain started to fall, and as the seeds got wet, they began to grow. Then the sun came out and got them warm, and they grew even faster. The acorn was growing faster than the pine.

As they grew older, the acorn had grown into a mighty oak tree with branches reaching as far as you could see, way up into the sky.

The little pine didn't grow very much, because he was in the shadow of the great oak tree. The rain and the sunlight didn't get to him as easily, since the overbearing oak grabbed it all.

All of the animals in the woods came to see the mighty oak, to play on its large branches, and to sit under its cool shade.

That poor little pine tree never had anyone play on his small branches. He felt very much alone.

Bob Morgan

Then, one day, the little pine saw all the animals scurrying about, as if they were frightened.

"What's the matter?" the little pine asked one scared little squirrel.

"Haven't you heard?" said the squirrel, "There is a bad storm coming, and I have to find some place to hide."

Oh, no! thought the little pine, *I am so small, I'm sure the wind will blow me away. I wish I could hide, too.*

"Ha! Ha! Look at me," the mighty oak said. "Look at my branches. I am big and strong, I have no reason to be afraid of the wind."

And then the wind came, and it blew very hard. It blew so hard, that the big, mighty oak blew over, and away. But the little pine held on. It didn't know it, but all during the time the mighty oak was spreading its mighty branches, it was not spending enough time putting down deep roots, which would have held him to the ground during that great windstorm.

The little pine was not growing big branches, but was growing a great deep root, so the windstorm could not pull him out of the ground.

After the wind and the rain went away, the little pine realized that he was getting taller and taller.

The shade from the mighty oak was not there anymore, and the sun was now shining directly onto that proud little pine.

The little pine grew and grew, until one day it was taller than any other tree in the forest. All of the animals from the forest came to play on its mighty branches, and sit under its cool shade.

And the mighty pine let them play in its cool shade, so long as they promised not to step on the little tree trying to grow way down below, or to block out its sun

So you see, every tree, every animal, and every kid, grow at a different rate. Some of you grow faster, some grow slower, but just because someone becomes bigger sooner, does not mean the person will be stronger in the long run. Also, it's important to allow everyone around you to get their share of the sun, don't you think?

Good night.

Bob Morgan

TWO SEEDS
THE MIGHTY OAK AND THE LITTLE PINE

28

THE HUMMINGBIRD

Once, in the woods not too far from where you and I live, there lived a hummingbird. Oh, she was a pretty bird, with red feathers on her neck, white feathers on her tail, and dark green feathers on her back. She was a real beauty. She was actually the prettiest hummingbird in the entire county. Even hummingbirds from the next county over, would come by just to see her. Do you want to know what her name was?

Well, her name was Sandra. But she never liked that name. She was a tomboy. She didn't play with dolls, or girl things. She was a very pretty girl, but girl toys bored her. She wanted everyone to call her "Sam."

Now, everything about Sam was pretty, except for one thing. Have you ever heard of a hummingbird that couldn't hum? Well, you have now. Sam couldn't hum like all of the other hummingbirds. Sam couldn't even sing like a regular bird.

Whenever she tried to hum, the sound she made was horrible. You would have to put your hands over your ears. It sounded like a trumpet! That's how bad her singing and humming was. But Sam never got upset over

29

not being able to hum. She would just sit in the treetops, listening to all the other birds singing and humming along, as they flew about all day. It was quite lovely.

Sam was a friendly hummingbird, so all of the other birds liked her. She had lots and lots of friends.

One day, everyone was in the woods eating lunch. The hummingbirds were getting nectar from the flowers, and the other birds were finding seeds and berries to eat. It was a very peaceful day until…a huge alley cat showed up.

Now, cats love to eat birds, and Sam knew this. She was the first to see the cat sneaking up on the other birds. She knew that she didn't have the time to fly over to warn the other birds to get up into the trees, high up, where it would be safe from the cat. And the cat was slinking closer and closer to Sam's friends. The only thing that she could do was, yep, try to hum and warn the other birds!

Well, you know that noise that Sam made trying to hum? It plumb scared that cat so badly, that he didn't stop running until he got well into the next county. And that cat never came back.

Now, even though it was a very scary and dangerous moment for the birds, when they saw what happened, they could not help thinking it was very funny, watching that cat skee-daddle. Sam thought it was funny, too. They all laughed about that scaredy-cat for a long time.

And don't you know, from then on the other birds brought nectar to Sam to pay her for sitting up in the treetops, and to be their watchbird, so that they wouldn't have to worry about cats, or any other animals, ever again!

And with that voice, Sam made a great watchbird. Would you like for Sam to sing a lullaby for you so you can drift off to sleep? No? Scaredy-cat.

Good night.

Bob Morgan

LUTHER,
THE LITTLE RED WAGON

When he was brand new, Luther was a proud little
wagon. He had a shiny body, with brightly colored
wheels. His handle was long, and painted a beautiful
black color. Every time someone walked by, Luther
would hold his head up proudly. He was such a
sparkling, spanking-new, super looking wagon.

But, all Luther did all day long was to sit in the front
yard. No one ever came by to play with him. He always
wondered, *Why, why, oh why don't the kids play with me?*
He thought that maybe the kids just didn't like him.
Luther knew that he had never done anything to make
the kids mad at him. He always had a smile on his face,
his paint was always sparkly, his wheels were always
bright. *Why won't they play with me*, Luther wondered?

Day after day, night after night, and finally, year after
year, poor Luther sat in that front yard all by himself,
having no one to play with. He didn't know that the kids
were in the house playing with their video games,
computers, and all the other types of new-fangled *inside*
toys.

32

Now, Stephine and Sean were a sister and brother who lived in the house attached to the yard where Luther lived. Stephine and Sean loved to play video games, but they finally became bored with them. So, that day they decided to go outside to play. That was a very good thing to do, because they really needed to get some fresh air, sunshine, and exercise.

As they were walking toward Luther, and they came closer to him, the more excited Luther became.

Oh boy, they are coming to play with me, he thought. But no, they walked right on past him on their way down the hill, to play in a pond that Luther had never been to play in. Poor Luther! No one likes to play with him.

And now that Luther had been sitting outdoors for so many years, he was not beautiful anymore. His shiny body was not shiny any more. It was now rusty. His once wonderful wheels were now squeaky, and ugly. His long slender handle had no black paint left on it. Luther wasn't proud, anymore.

Sean and Stephine were down by the pond having a good time. They were skipping flat stones across the water, watching them skip along the surface, sometimes two, or even three times. They had forgotten how much fun it was to play outside!

All of a sudden, Stephine stepped on a sharp rock. The rock was so sharp, that it cut through her shoe, and right into her foot.

"Oh my, that hurts," she cried. "I can't walk on it. How am I going to get back home?"

Now, Sean couldn't leave her there all by herself while he went for help. And Stephine was too big to carry up that hill.

"What are we going to do," they both cried?

Luther was watching them that whole time, and knew that he had to do something to help.

I know, I know, I know what to do, he thought. With all of his strength, he made his rusty handle turn towards the kids. Then he made his creaky old wheels go forward a little, then a little more, and soon he was on his way down that old hill. But boy, was he making a lot of squeaking, rattling, and groaning noises. At last, he made it all the way to the two kids.

"Quick," he told Sean, "Put Stephine on me, and the two of us together can wheel her back up that big, nasty, old hill." Luther stood perfectly still, while Sean put Stephine carefully onto his back. Then, with a heave and a ho, a squeak and a squow, they started pushing Stephine up that big hill.

In hardly any time at all, they had Stephine into the house, with her mother taking care of her foot. It wasn't really serious, so their mother had Stephine feeling much better in just a few minutes.

"It just looks worse than it is," she told them. Stephine was glad that her mother was there, and so was Sean.

"I think that we should do something nice for the wagon, don't you, Stephine?" asked Sean?

"Yes, I certainly do," said Stephine, "He really helped us out today, I don't know what we would have done without him."

Stephine and Sean asked their dad to get them some black paint, some bright red paint, and some sparkling, white paint. They said "We have an idea!"

First, they took off all of Luther's rust. Next, they painted him! Luther's new paint job was even more beautiful than the original paint had been, when he had been brand new. And boy, was he a pretty wagon once again!

Stephine and Sean don't play very many indoor video or computer games anymore.

Can you guess why? They just don't have the time. They are too busy playing outside with their shiny, happy, proud little wagon.

Good night!

Bob Morgan

LUTHER, THE LITTLE RED WAGON

THE FUNNY AARDVARK FAMILY

This is the story about the very first aardvark family. My great-great-grandfather told this story to me when I was about your age. He said that the story was true, and I have no reason to doubt it. After watching aardvarks today, I believe it even more. Here is what he told me, and exactly the way he told me this story.

The very first aardvark family lived very far away from where you and I live. There was the mother named Rita, and the father named Gene, and a son and a daughter. Their names were Hank and Toni.

They had a beautiful home on the beach. They all loved the beach. Gene and Rita, and Hank and Toni, were all very pretty aardvarks. Now, with their beautiful home on the beach, and all of them being very pretty, you would think this was the perfect happy family, wouldn't you? I would have thought so, too.

Well, there was a problem. A very big problem! Rita could not cook. She tried and tried, but all of her meals were awful. She tried to make biscuits one day and, well, the whole family asked her not to do that again! The biscuits were terrible. But at least Toni and Hank could use them to play baseball with, that's how hard they turned out.

One day, Rita tried to cook grits, and they turned out so awful that the whole family was scared to even try them. But, you know what? Gene took all of the grits out to his sidewalk, and when the grits dried they made a nice walkway. The grits became even harder than the cement he had been using!

Now Rita was a very sweet aardvark. Her family loved her very much. All of the neighbors loved her, too. But when anyone came to visit, they would always bring along their own food! Everybody knew that Rita could not cook! But everyone, including Rita, thought it was so funny, and laughed about it all the time.

Well, one day, Rita made up her mind that she was going to make the perfect meal for her family. She stayed in the kitchen all day cooking that meal. When it came suppertime, Gene, Hank, and Toni came in and boy, were they getting hungry by now. Rita, Gene, Toni, and Hank all took one bite of the supper, and agreed they had never tasted anything that awful before. They ran over to the window, and each one threw the meal out onto the ground outside.

Rita said to her family, "I'm so sorry, but I will never be able to cook well!" The whole family told her that it was alright, and that they loved her anyhow. And they really did!

After the food had been on the ground for a few minutes, guess who came to visit? The same insects that come to visit every time we leave food outside! Can you guess who it was? Ants! Millions of ants!

As you children might imagine, by now that first aardvark family was pretty well starving. None of Momma Rita's meals had ever worked out, and snacking isn't the same as having a real meal.

Well, Gene took one look at the ants and thought, "*Say, they might taste pretty good.*" He took one in his mouth and ate it! "*Wow, this thing is delicious!*" He got the whole family to try them, and they all loved them.

So, Gene and Rita and Hank and Toni never had to worry about momma Rita's terrible cooking ever again, because there were always plenty of ants around.

Now children, even up until today, there never was an aardvark that could cook! And my great-great grandfather told me that is why we call aardvarks the "Great Anteaters."

I believe that this story is probably true, don't you?

Good night.

Bob Morgan

THE FUNNY AARDVARKS EATING ANTS

COUNT TO TEN

1- Let's use your thumb for number ONE. So stick up your thumb on your left hand. ONE stands for the ONE and only ONE time will you be born. It is only ONE life, so let's make the most of it. To help you grow up to be a very good person, hug your mommy and daddy, and sister and brother each and every day. Then tell them that you love them, and you know what? They will love you right back!

2- Let's use your index finger for number TWO. Do you know where your index finger is? Ask your parents and they will tell you, or just look right next to your thumbs. TWO stands for the only parents you will ever have. So make them proud of you by being a good little girl or boy. You can learn how to do that by doing what number ONE says.

3- Let's use the middle finger for number THREE. The middle finger is the one next to the index finger. Are you still using your left hand? Good! Here we go! THREE stands for the number of people that makes up your family. Count them. Mommy, daddy, and you. Is that THREE?

4- Let's use the ring finger for number FOUR. Ask your mommy which finger is the ring finger, or look right next to your pinkies. FOUR stands for the number of living people in your family, if you have a brother or sister. Are there FOUR in your family?

5- Let's use the pinky finger for number FIVE. Do you know where the pinky finger is? It is the only finger that is not sticking up on your left hand. FIVE stands for the number of living beings in your family, if you have a brother and a pet. Do you have a pet? Are all of your fingers sticking up on your left hand?

6- Let's use the other hand now. It is called the right hand. Stick up your thumb on your right hand, and it will stand for SIX. If you had a brother and a sister, as well as a pet, then you would have SIX members in your family. Do you have SIX members in your family?

7- Let's use the index finger on this hand to stand for SEVEN. If you had a brother and TWO sisters, and a pet, then you would have SEVEN members in your family. Do you have SEVEN members in your family? It would be a large family.

8- Now stick up your middle finger, and we will call that EIGHT. If you have TWO brothers, TWO sisters, and a kitten, then you will have EIGHT members in your family. Is your family as big as that?

9- Stick up your other ring finger, and we will call that NINE. If you have TWO brothers, TWO sisters, a kitten and a dog, then you would have NINE members in your family. Now that would be a really large family.

10- There is only ONE finger left to stick up. It is the pinky again. If you stick that one up, then you will have TEN. Do you know what would be a good thing to stand for TEN? I do!

Each and every day,
give your mommy and daddy,
and every member of your family
TEN hugs!

We will stop now because we don't have any more fingers to count with. Do you want to look down at your feet, and we can count your toes? Maybe tomorrow night...

Good night.

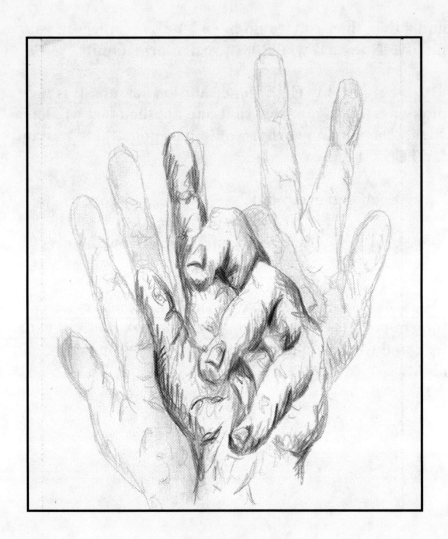

COUNT TO TEN

A GREEN BALLOON

The little green balloon sat on the store shelf, feeling different. All his friends were bright, red, shiny, balloons.

Little boys and girls always came into the store, but never picked the little green balloon to take home, or to share their birthday parties with, and such. They always picked those beautiful red balloons.

Whenever this happened, the little green balloon felt sad. He sat in the store all day trying to look happy, so that the little kids would choose him. But at night, when the store was closed and no one was around, that little green balloon would cry himself to sleep.

Each new day, when the store would open again, the little green balloon would try to put a smile on his face. But it was very hard to do.

The owner of the store looked at the poor green balloon and said, "No one is ever going to buy you, so I guess I will just put you on a shelf in the back of the store."

The little green balloon thought, *at least it will be dark back there, so no one will see me crying!*

One day a lady came into the store and said, "I want a lot of balloons for my son's birthday."

The storeowner said, "Okay, I'll go to the back of the store and get a big box to put them all in."

It was so dark in the back of the store that the owner accidentally bumped into the shelf, and knocked the little green balloon into the box. The little green balloon worried about what was going to happen to him.

The storeowner filled the box with red balloons and handed them to the lady, never noticing that the little green balloon was in there too, and that he was very scared.

That night the lady started blowing up all the balloons. Then she came upon our friend, the green balloon.

"Well, just how did you get in there?" she asked. "Oh well, you are so cute that I'll just blow you up too!"

After he was blown up (which felt very strange), the little green balloon just rolled into a corner and hid. He felt so different from the rest!

All of the children who came to the birthday party were having fun with the bunch of red balloons. The little green balloon sat in the corner by himself and listened to all of the fun, wishing he could join them. But he felt different and scared.

After a while, the kids became bored with just the red balloons.

A little boy saw the little green balloon, and said "Why are you hiding in this corner? Come on out here and play with us."

"Oh, look! A pretty green balloon!" exclaimed all of the other kids. And soon they all took turns playing with him for the rest of the party.

The birthday boy's mother asked "Why were you hiding? Don't you know that being different makes you very special? You are definitely the one I would have chosen to play with!"

And so the little green balloon realized how special being different was, and that he would never have to be upset or cry about it again!

Good night.

A PORCUPINE NAMED PRESTON

Preston was just a little porcupine. You see, he wasn't very old. He was just about as old as you are. But, he had a lot more quills than his mommy or daddy had. Do you know what a quill is?

As you might imagine, Preston Porcupine had a terrible time getting a hug from his mommy or daddy, since their quills would cause them to stick each other, every time the family tried to hug! Aren't you glad that you are not a porcupine? So each time his parents wanted to hug him, especially at night when he was being tucked into bed, they would have to blow each other kisses, instead.

That sure seems the best way for porcupines to show that they love each other, don't you think?

During the daytime, poor Preston had no friends to play with, because of his quills. Oh, how he wished that he had a brother or sister to play with. But Preston lived in the forest, and the only creatures who lived there were other birds and animals, but no other porcupines.

One day, Preston became so lonely, that he just started walking. And he walked. And he walked some more. Eventually, he came upon a very big city. He could see people scrambling about everywhere. He could see cars going in every direction. And Preston could see a sandlot full of litter, with lots of kids standing nearby, looking into it.

They seemed to be staring into that filthy sandlot, thinking very deeply about what to do in that lot.

Preston didn't know what to think of the kids, because he had never seen any children before. However, they all seemed friendly enough.

Then he heard one of the kids say, "Look at all of the paper and trash all over this lot," Preston listened very carefully to what the kids were saying. "If it were clean, then we would have a nice place to play. But we are not big enough to clean it up!"

"I know," said one little boy, who had bright red hair. "I will get my mommy and daddy to help, and we will have it cleaned up in no time at all!"

Well, by now it was getting pretty late, and Preston decided that he had better hurry home, so that his mommy and daddy wouldn't be worried about him. Off he ran as fast as he could go. And Preston got home just in time for dinner, too. He fell asleep soon after dinner, wondering how he could help the kids in that empty, trashy, sandlot.

The next day, after he had eaten a nice breakfast, and brushed his teeth, Preston ran back to the sandlot really fast, so he could help the kids. He didn't know how he could help, he just knew that he would. What he saw when he arrived at the sandlot made him feel very sad. There were no parents to help the kids clean up the sandlot. All of the parents were at work, and could not come to help.

Preston wished that he could help, somehow! When he saw one little girl crying, he just knew that he had to do something, this very minute! Seeing her so sad made him want to cry, too. Then he thought of a way that might help those kids! Now, you are not going to believe this, but he did something that I have never seen a porcupine do. I have never seen any of the other animals do it, either.

Preston rolled himself up into a ball. Then he went rolling down the hill, and you should have seen those quills sticking into the paper and the trash that was all over the sandlot! Little Preston rolled, and rolled, until he had picked up all of the trash in the sandlot. Then he rolled over to the garbage can, jumped on top of the can, and shook himself very hard. All of that paper and trash fell off of him, and went right into the garbage can.

As you can imagine, all of the kids were thrilled. They were so happy with Preston, that they asked him to play ball with them. They wanted him to be their newest, best friend!

Preston Porcupine played and played with the kids all day, being very careful not to touch them. It was the best day that he could ever remember. He not only found a friend, but he found a lot of friends, all in one single day!

That night, when it was time for all the kids to go home, they all wanted to hug Preston. But Preston told them, "No, I can't let you hug me, because I like you too much, you wouldn't want to get stuck by my quills...blow me a kiss, instead." And they all did.

Give your mommy and daddy a big hug for Preston, because you don't have quills!

Good night.

PRESTON PORCUPINE

CLAYTON, THE CLYDESDALE

When Clayton was just a young horse, all he could ever think about was wanting to be like his daddy. Now, his daddy was a big powerful horse, and he was so handsome. All of the other horses wanted to be just like him, too.

Clayton's daddy could pull the heaviest loads without even trying. And when he stood alone on the hillside in the pasture, he was a beautiful sight to see. He was so big and tall, and everyone just wanted to look at him.

His mane was dark brown. His tail was a light brown, and his back was almost gray. He had huge hooves, as all Clydesdales do. But his big hooves just made him look even more handsome. He could do just about anything.

Clayton would get so mad at himself, because he could not do all the things that his daddy could do. But Clayton had no way of knowing that someday, he would be just as handsome, and even stronger than his daddy. He only had to wait until he grew up a little more.

One day, the owner of the ranch where Clayton lived came by in his shiny new car. It was a very nice car, with a roof that folded back, which made it look like a racing car. It was also very pretty when the top was down, too.

It had rained earlier that day, and all of the roads were slippery and muddy. That shiny new car really got dirty in all of that mud. And then it happened! The new car became stuck in the mud.

"Oh boy," the owner said, "What am I going to do now?"

Clayton saw him getting stuck in the mud, and ran down the hillside as fast as he could, to see if he could help.

"I'll pull you out of the mud," Clayton said to the owner.

The owner smiled and said, "Thank you, but I think that you are bit too small to pull this big car out of the mud!"

"Let me try, let me try," Clayton said to the owner.

"I will let you try," said the owner, "But I don't want you to be disappointed if you can't, because I think you just may not be big enough yet!"

Clayton pulled and tugged, and tugged and pulled some more, but that car just would not budge from that sticky old mud!

"Go home, Clayton, and ask your father if he would come and help me," said the owner. "And don't feel badly about not being able to pull the car out of the mud. You are just too young, and too small, to do things like that! But one day you will be able to do it!"

Clayton didn't know it, but one day he would be able to pull two cars out of the mud, both at the same time!

Clayton ran home just as fast as his little legs would carry him. "Daddy, Daddy, the owner's car is stuck in the mud, and he needs for you to come help him!"

Clayton's daddy ran over to the muddy road, and found the owner's car still bogged down in the slippery mud. The owner tied a rope to Clayton's daddy, and with a mighty heave, he pulled that car right out of that mudhole as if there were nothing to it.

Wow, I hope that I can do that one day, Clayton thought. He was so proud of his father!

When Clayton and his father got home that night, Clayton asked him, "How did you get to be so big and strong?"

"Well, son, if you watch what I eat each day, and eat what I do, it will help you get big and strong, too," he said.

So Clayton started watching his daddy very closely. For breakfast, Clayton grabbed a doughnut. Clayton's daddy got some healthy cereal from the pantry. Clayton decided that he wanted to be just like his daddy, so he had better eat the same things. He threw that doughnut right into the garbage can.

That day at lunch time, Clayton grabbed a hamburger. Clayton's daddy ate some fruits and vegetables. So, off into the garbage can went that fatty hamburger!

That night for supper, Clayton grabbed a pizza. Clayton's daddy had corn on the cob. Guess what Clayton did with that pizza? And guess what Clayton had for supper?

In no time at all, Clayton was getting bigger and stronger. One day he looked at his daddy, and you know what? Clayton was just a little bit taller than his daddy. He was also getting to be quite handsome. His mane was getting browner, and his tail was getting very long and brown, and his back was turning into that pretty gray color! Clayton was growing up!

And then, one day, the rain started coming down again. The roads became even muddier than before. And guess what got stuck in the mud? The shiny new car? Nope. A great big, huge truck!

Clayton's father said, "Well, I guess I had better get down there and see if I can help."

Clayton looked at his father and said calmly, "Please let me try."

"Ok son, I think you are ready," said his dad, "Do you think that I should help you?"

"No, father, I need to do this by myself," said Clayton.

Clayton's father knew that Clayton could do it all by himself, and he watched him go down the hill and pull that big old truck out of the mud. It seemed like Clayton didn't even have to try hard!

You know, Clayton's father thought to himself, *I don't think I was ever strong enough to pull something that big out of the mud.*

Now, when Clayton stands on the hillside all alone, with his long mane blowing in the wind, and looking so powerful and handsome, his father thinks to himself, *Wow!* And he is very proud of his son, Clayton.

Good night.

ETHEL THE EARTHWORM

This story is going to be about something yucky! Can you guess what that might be? Our story is about an earthworm named Ethel.

Now, no one likes earthworms, right? They are slimy and nasty looking. Do you like to hold earthworms in your hand? I didn't think so. Do you like to eat earthworms? Yuck! I don't!

So, earthworms are really not good for anything. Right? WRONG!

A girl named Kristie lives near Ethel Earthworm's hole-in-the-ground. Kristie is a pretty girl, and loves to grow things in her garden. The trouble is that Kristie can never get anything to grow in her garden. All of her flowers die. All of her fruits and vegetables die, and always before she has a chance to pick them. She tries and tries to grow things, but nothing seems to like to grow in her garden. She didn't know what was wrong.

One day Kristie found a book on how to grow a garden. The book told her how to grow just about everything.

Did you know that no matter what kind of problem you may have, you can probably find out how to fix it by reading "how to…" in a book? Yes, there are even books on how to grow a garden!

It seems like Kristie's problem was that the dirt was packed too tightly. She needed something that could loosen the soil, so the roots from her plants could grow more easily, and make beautiful plants.

Kristie thought and thought about how to loosen the soil in her garden. Nothing that she tried would ever work. She badly wanted to see her garden grow.

Now, here is where that old, useless, slimy worm comes into our story. What did I say her name was? Oh yes, Ethel! Ethel Earthworm heard about Kristie's problem, and she knew how to fix it. You see, earthworms bore holes in the soil all day long, and sometimes at nighttime, too. And Ethel is an excellent borer. The holes she puts into the soil let air in, and also keep the soil nice and loose.

And do you know happens when the ground is very loose, and you plant vegetables or fruit? That's right! They will grow and grow and get to be very beautiful. That is what is about to happen to Kristie's garden.

One day Ethel found herself all the way over into Kristie's garden. She was so busy boring holes that she didn't notice that Kristie was watching her. She kept on boring and boring holes, until all that soil was very loose.

Kristie saw what Ethel was doing, and loved her for it. All of the machines that Kristie had in her barn could not loosen the soil like Ethel was doing. And Ethel Earthworm was doing it all for free! Also, Ethel was getting her food from the soil as she was boring the holes. That is just how earthworms get their food.

Not too long after that, Kristie planted some of her favorite vegetables, and her favorite fruit. She would go outside every morning to see if the plants had come up yet. She could hardly wait! Then one day she woke up and ran outside, and the garden was just beautiful with all of the green colors. And those plants grew and grew, until all of the vegetables were just right to pick. The fruit tree was ready, too! That was the first time that Kristie ever picked a vegetable from her own garden, and boy, was it good! She had fresh fruits and vegetables forevermore.

Kristie tried and tried to find Ethel to thank her. But by this time, Ethel was in another part of town making someone else very happy. Kristie was so very glad that Ethel came to her yard; but, Kristie came to realize that Ethel, and her entire family of millions of earthworms, must continue traveling through the soil, making things better as they go.

So, the next time you are eating one of your favorite vegetables, just think, a slimy, yucky-old earthworm helped grow this. And, you know, it might have even been Ethel!

Good night.

KRISTIE WATCHES ETHEL THE EARTHWORM

NO, WE DIDN'T LOSE

Bryan loved to play softball. He had three friends who loved to play softball, too. Collin was one of Bryan's friends. Travis and Andrew were two more of Bryan's friends, who loved to play the game just as much as Bryan and Collin. Have you ever played softball?

Bryan and his friends loved to play softball against some other teams in his hometown. One team was really, really good, and it sure wasn't Bryan's team! That very good team had beaten most of the other teams in their town, but Bryan's team had not yet played against them.

One day, Collin said to Bryan, "Why don't we invite that good team over for a game? I know we can beat them, and it sure would be fun to try!"

"Yes, I think we can beat them, too," Bryan said.

The good team's name was The Terrible Tigers, and they had that name for a good reason. On the softball field, they played like tigers, wanting fiercely to win each and every game that they played. They were a very good team, because they had a coach. Do you know what a coach is? What does a coach do?

Andrew, another friend of Bryan's, decided to go watch The Terrible Tigers practice one day, just to see what made them so good. He saw the reason…the coach!

So, he thought to himself, *we need a coach, too. A coach can show us the right way to hit the ball, and the right way to pitch the ball. I'll go tell my friends that we need a coach. Then we can win all of our games!*

It just so happened that Travis' dad was a high school softball coach. What luck! Travis asked his dad, Scotty, if he would coach the team.

"Of course I will," Scotty said, "I would be happy to coach your team."

Well, those boys started practicing, with Scotty's help. They practiced and practiced. Then, when they weren't doing their homework, they practiced even more!

They practiced after school.
They practiced on weekends.
They even practiced on holidays.

Those kids really worked hard practicing their softball skills.

Finally, the time came when they felt that they could beat The Terrible Tigers! Bryan invited them over to play a game, the next Saturday afternoon at three o'clock. The Terrible Tigers accepted the invitation.

Oh boy, this should be a really good game!

Bryan couldn't wait until Saturday. He was so excited!
All day Friday he and his Mom, Rebecca, and his Dad,
Derek, practiced with him so he would be ready for the
big game.

Saturday came. Bryan and his parents went to the
ballpark. There, he met all of his friends. They were all
ready. Their uniforms were as clean as a whistle. Their
shoes were spotless. Their softball gloves were shiny.
They were ready.

The Terrible Tigers came out and boy, did they look
ready, too! It sure looked like Bryan's team was going to
have to play hard to win this game.

The Tigers went to bat first. The first batter hit the ball
really hard, but Travis was ready for it, and caught it
with one hand. One out!

The second batter came up to home plate. He really
smacked that ball, and he made it to first base...man on
first, one out.

The third batter came up. He struck out. Out two! The
fourth batter came up to the plate. He hit that ball so
hard that the bat broke in not one, but two places. A
home run! Two runs for the Tigers, still two out!

The next batter came up, and he struck out. Out three!

Now it was time for Bryan and his teammates to show what they could do. Bryan came up to bat first. The Tiger's pitcher threw the ball so fast, that Bryan didn't even see it…strike one. Again it happened. Then again! Bryan struck out, out number one!

Next, Travis came up to bat. He swung the bat, and missed the ball.
        Strike one.   Strike two.   Strike three!
Travis struck out also, out number two.

Then Andrew came up to bat. He hit the ball, and it zipped right past the pitcher. Andrew made it all the way around to second base, a double, with two out!

Scotty put Bryan back up to bat, and told him to look out for that fast pitch. Bryan did. He was more careful this time up. He had his eyes on that ball, from the time it left the pitcher's hand. When the ball came within striking distance, Bryan hit it with all of his strength. He knocked it deep into center field. Andrew made it to home plate to score the first run for his team. Bryan also made it all the way around to home plate, to score the second run! Two runs for Bryan's team, two runs for the Tigers, a tie score!

One of the other boys came up to bat.
        Strike one.   Strike two.   Strike three!
Three outs, sides retired, the Tigers come up to bat next.

The game was tied, and this kind of excitement went on all afternoon. Both teams played their hardest. They both played as well as they could. It was a really good, close game!

Then, in the last inning, with the score tied, it was the Tigers' time to bat. Bryan's team could not let them score a point. If they did, the game was over, and The Terrible Tigers would win!

The first batter came up, and stood there, waiting. The pitcher tossed the ball, the batter hit it, and started running towards first base. Travis grabbed the ball, and threw it to Andrew, a good fielding effort. But the ball got there too late, the batter was already safely on first base!

The second batter came up, and he was the same player who had broken his bat getting the home run early in the game. The pitcher threw the ball as fast as he could. The batter looked worried for a moment, but then whammed that ball completely out of the ballpark! Two more runs score, and The Terrible Tigers win the game.

Now, you may be wondering why Bryan's team didn't win in this story. After all, the name of the story is, "No, We Didn't Lose."

Well, my advice to you is:
Read the rest of the story!

The Terrible Tigers' whole team, with the coach, came over to talk with Scotty, Bryan, and the rest of their team. They looked worn, tired and terrible!

The captain of the Tigers announced to Bryan's whole team, "We have never played a team like yours. You tried your hearts out, and you really made us work harder than any other team ever has. With the way you practiced to play us, and all of the work you put in trying to beat us, you are going to have an outstanding team. Just keep it up, and next year when we play you again, you will most probably beat us! And, you know, the way both teams played today, no matter what the final score was, no one really lost!"

On his way home that Saturday night, Bryan thought about what good sportsmanship it took for the Tigers' team to come over to tell them how they felt about the game. He thought, *they're right, today there were no losers…* and then he thought *…the Tigers were champions in more ways than one!*

Good night.

I WISH I COULD TALK

I wish that I could talk, but I can't, for you see, I am a larva. I can hear, and I can think, but I cannot talk. So please, don't talk about me. That is so unkind! Also, I am really nice, if I think so, myself. I even have a beautiful name...I think of myself as Renee.

Most people look at me, and think that I am not pretty. Do you think I am not pretty? After all, I am just something that looks like a worm. But, I can hear, so please do not talk about me.

I see a beautiful ballerina. When I see her dancing with those soft, graceful moves, I wish that I could talk, and tell her how beautiful I think she is. Wait, she is walking towards me! Maybe she will notice me. She has!

"Oh, what an ugly worm," I hear her say. "I am so glad that I am a beautiful ballerina, instead of that ugly worm!"

Oh, if only that ballerina could somehow know how I feel inside, then she would see that I am pretty, too, I thought.

I sure wish that I could talk!

I see an ice skater gliding across the ice, as if she is floating. I think that she is beautiful. I wish that I could talk to her, and tell her how I wish that I could glide across the ice! But I can never tell her that, since, as you know, I can't speak. Look, she is skating towards me! Maybe she will notice me! She has!

"Oh my, what is something like you doing in here?" she asked. What the ice skater said wasn't very nice.

That ice skater may be beautiful on the outside, but her thoughts are not very pretty, I thought.

I wish that I could talk!

I see a man and his daughter. I see they are laughing, and hugging each other. I know that they love each other. Maybe they are nice. I hope that they notice me! Wait, they are walking towards me! They did see me!

The daughter saw me first. "Look, daddy! Look at this pretty worm," she says. The daddy looked at Renee.

Why yes, that is a very pretty worm, he thought. They both loved all birds and animals, and yes, even insects, which is what a Larva is. The father and daughter thought all living creatures were beautiful!

"My name is Clay," said the father. "What is your name?"

"My name is Brenda," said the little girl.

"What can we call you?"

Oh, how I wish that I could talk. I would tell Clay and Brenda that I think they are very nice, and I would tell them my name!

How I wish that I could talk!

Wait! Something is happening to me! I am changing! I am changing into something completely different! I feel so different now!

Look, I have changed into a beautiful butterfly! Look at my wings of silk. I am lighter than the breeze. I can fly! I can flutter above the treetops. I can drink the sweet nectar from all the lovely flowers that I see.

I see the ballerina. She sees me! I hear her say that she wishes that she could be as beautiful as me. But she can never be, because her thoughts are not nice, and that is what really makes someone beautiful!

I see the ice skater. She sees me! I hear her say that she wishes that she could be as pretty as me. But she will never be! She has many unkind thoughts, and that would prevent her from being as beautiful as me!

I see Clay and Brenda. They see me! They always thought that I was beautiful. They have very kind thoughts. They would never hurt my feelings. They are too full of love to ever hurt anything. I love them, too. They are beautiful!

I see now that I really don't want to talk! I don't need to! I was happy when I was a larva, because I was beautiful inside. How sad that some people could not see that!

Now that I am a butterfly, I will fly all over, and somehow let other larva know that I think they are beautiful, too!

I am glad that I don't feel the need to talk anymore!

Here are two flutters of my silky wings…which is butterfly talk for…

Good night.

SISSY,
THE PINK, CLEAN, LITTLE PIG

Sissy was a little pig that just didn't like mud. Now, I bet you thought that all pigs love to play in the mud, didn't you? Well, I did too, until I met little Sissy.

Now, I can be the one telling you this story, because I was there when this all happened. My name is Randy, and I am a pig, too. But, I am a pig that is like most other pigs. I love to root around in the mud. I love feeling mud on my feet. I love feeling mud on my back, and I really love feeling mud on my snout!

I know that all of you who read my story will be human people, so I will tell you what a snout is. It is the thing that sticks out on my face. You humans would call it a nose. Actually, I think that you human people look funny with your noses sticking out the human way they do, but that is another story!

All of Sissy's friends would ask her to come out and play in the mud with them, but Sissy would not do that. Sissy loved to stay indoors, and to take long, warm, bubble-baths. Yes, baths! Sissy was a very clean pig. She would put polish on her hooves. She would use a nice shampoo

71

on her hair. And, I must admit, for a pig she certainly did smell good!

One day I was out playing in the mud with my jump-rope. You must be wondering what in the world a pig is doing with a jump-rope, especially in the mud? Well, pigs like to play with toys, just like humans do. And I happen to like my jump-rope, even splishy-splashy in the mud!

I was having a really good time that day, jumping up and down, skipping with my jump-rope in all that mud. Then it happened. I jumped up, and came down with the rope tangled around my feet, somehow. I couldn't get that jump-rope loose! So there I was in the mud, with my feet all tangled up in my jump-rope and I couldn't move. I was in really big trouble!

I squealed for help, but no one heard me. I squealed some more, and how I wished that someone would come by to help me. I was getting pretty tired by then, and I didn't know what I was going to do. Finally, I opened my mouth and let out the loudest *squeal* you have ever heard!

Sissy heard me, and she knew that I was in trouble by that loud squeal. She came running as fast as her little, porker legs would carry her!

"Don't worry, Randy, I will untie that jump-rope," she shouted. And do you know what? Sissy jumped right into that mud, and she untied that jump-rope from my feet! Boy, was I ever glad that she helped me!

"Sissy," I asked, "I know that you don't like the mud, so how come you jumped in to help me?"

"I jumped in to help you because you are a friend of mine, and that is what friends are for, to help each other," she told me. Now, Sissy and I are better friends than ever!

You may be wondering if Sissy likes playing in the mud now, after that. Nope! Right after she helped me that day, she went straight home, and she took another long, warm, bubble-bath, put polish on her hooves, and used that sweet smelling shampoo on her hair!

All of the other little pigs don't mind that Sissy doesn't like playing in the mud, because she is just so sweet, they all like her. As for me, I loved Sissy even before she helped me, and I love her even more now...even though she doesn't like playing around in the mud. I mean, what is wrong with a good-smelling pig?

Now, close your eyes, and try to smell Sissy's sweet smelling bubble-bath and shampoo...can you smell them? And, "oink, snort," which, as you know in pig-talk means...

Good night.

SISSY, THE PINK, CLEAN, LITTLE PIG

LOGAN, THE LIZARD

Logan was a pretty special lizard. Some lizards can change colors anytime they want to. Logan could too, he just could do it faster than the other lizards. Do you know what you would call a lizard that can change colors? Ask the person reading this story to you what they are called. Are you big enough to read this story all by yourself? Do you know what they are called? I will write it down for the little children who don't know what they are called, then. It is a very big word! Are you ready? They are called... are you sure that you are ready? Ok, they are called chameleons! That is a big word, isn't it?

Okay then, let's get back to our story. Logan lived in a town with lots and lots of other lizards. It was a very nice town, and was a very safe place for lizards to live. Lizards have to be very careful about where they live, because there are a lot of birds and animals that would love to have them for lunch. Well, as long as those lizards stayed in that town, they were safe!

Logan had a sister named Abigail. She was a pretty little lizard, and Logan loved her very much. And, of course, she loved Logan. They always played together in

75

the sand, and in the buildings, and in the water. They had lots and lots of friends, who liked to play along with them.

Logan woke up early one beautiful spring morning, and went out to play. He played for a long time, and then he began wondering why Abigail wasn't awake already and out playing with him. He ran back home, ran up the stairs, and saw his mother in Abigail's bedroom.

"What's wrong Mother? Why is Abigail still in bed?"

"She is terribly sick," said their mother, "I am very worried about her!"

Now, Logan's father just happened to be a doctor, which was very lucky! Logan's mother called his doctor daddy, and told him to come home, that Abigail was terribly sick! In just a few minutes, Logan's father came rushing into the bedroom! He felt her pulse, he checked her temperature, and did everything that he could to find out what was wrong with Abigail.

Then he turned around with a sad look on his face, "I know what is wrong, but the medicine she needs is in another town, a long way from here. I don't know how we can get the medicine back here safely!"

Logan already knew how they were going to get the medicine to his sister! He was going to go get it himself! He loved Abigail very much, and did not want anything bad to happen to her! He asked his father which town the medicine was in.

"Why do you want to know, son," the father asked?

"Because I am going to get it," said Logan.

"But you can't do that, it is too dangerous!"

"But father," Logan cried, "Don't forget, I can change colors faster than anybody! That will help me."

"Okay son, go, but please be very careful, there are a lot of animals and birds out there, and they will be looking for someone just like you to eat!"

So, saying bye-bye to his parents, Logan took off running just as fast as he could go. He ran into a forest where everything was green. He turned himself green right away! He came upon a lake and he had to swim across, so he turned himself blue just like the water. No one could see him!

Logan finally got to the town where the medicine was, he got the medicine, turned around, and just as quick as a wink, started running back towards home with the medicine for Abigail.

Suddenly, he found himself in a very sandy place which he had crossed on his way to the town. It seemed very safe that first time coming here. However, this time it was a bit different. This time there were hawks, and eagles, and crows flying above, looking for something to eat. And Logan was just the type of meal that they were looking for!

Bob Morgan

But why are you worried?

Did you forget that Logan could change colors very fast?

**Besides, we can't let anything happen to our hero,
can we?**

Logan was very worried about Abigail, so he looked
closely at the very light brown sand, studying the color.
Fast, what color do you think that Logan changed into?
You didn't say orange or purple, did you? I didn't think
so. In a wink, Logan changed into that same light brown
color, so that those dangerous, hungry birds would not
see him.

All of a sudden, he was in a place with green grass, but
you know what? Again, Logan changed colors so fast
that no one saw him do it! He was almost safely home now.

When he saw his home Logan ran even faster than ever
before, to get the medicine to his sister. His parents were
so glad that he was safe! Then, they quickly gave the
medicine to Abigail.

Later that same night, Abigail was feeling much better,
thanks to that dangerous trip that our hero, Logan
Lizard, accomplished safely!

The next day, Logan ran out into the yard to play, and
do you know, Abigail was there waiting for him. That
made Logan feel wonderful, having his sister to play with
again.

At the beginning of this story, you were probably thinking...

how in the world can a lizard be called a hero?

Well, now that you heard Logan's story, you know, don't you? Now close your eyes, and it'll be just like you're along with Logan, for that whole, color-changing journey.

Good night from one hero to another.

BURR, THE COCKLEBUR

In an open meadow, by a patch of beautiful flowers, lay a lonely seed named Burr. He wasn't a very pretty seed, and he had a hard time making friends. None of the flowers wanted Burr around, because he could never grow up to be as pretty as them.

Then, one day the wind started blowing, and it blew Burr into a garden of roses.

"Oh no," the pretty roses said, "We don't want you here, because you are not pretty enough!" The roses should have been ashamed of themselves for hurting Burr's feelings, don't you agree?

I wish the wind would blow me to a friendlier place, thought Burr. And, finally, it did!

The day that the wind started was one of those hot summer days. All of the animals and the birds were looking for some shade, so they could get cooler. The wind blew Burr to a great hillside, and as he rolled past a lovely flower, he asked, "May I stop by you?"

"No," the flower said, "I don't think you could ever be pretty enough to grow beside me." So poor Burr let himself roll further down the hill.

As Burr continued rolling down that hill, he saw a cute little tree. "May I stop by you?" he asked the cute little pine tree.

"No," said the tree, "I don't think you could ever be pretty enough to grow beside me!"

Then Burr rolled on, close to a rock. "May I stop by you," he asked?

"No," said the rock, "I don't think you could ever be pretty enough to live beside me!"

Burr began to think that he would never find a place to grow. *Maybe I am just too ugly to have a friend*, he thought, *No one wants me!* He was one sad little cocklebur seed!

As Burr rolled on down the hill, he heard a sound that he had heard many times before. It was the sound of someone crying! He looked around, and finally found who was crying. It was another little seed that looked so lonely!

"What's wrong," asked Burr?

"I am sad because I am a seed that cannot live in the hot sun. I have to have shade to live under," said the little seed.

Now Burr knew that someday he himself would be big and tall, and would make a big shade, just as his mother and father did!

"You can grow under my shade if you would care to, for I will be a big bush soon," Burr told the little seed.

And, as some gentle rain fell, and the sun shone down on the two, they started to grow. And they grew and grew!

The little lonely flower seed turned into a beautiful flower that all the other flowers were jealous of. They all wished that they could look like that flower!

And the beautiful little flower was proud of his big friend, Burr.

And Burr was proud of himself for helping such a lovely, friendly, warm, loving, plant grow! Burr and the beautiful flower say,

Good night.

I'LL DO IT TOMORROW

Amos was a little boy who wanted to wait until tomorrow to do just about everything.

He always thought that what he was doing was more important than anything he was supposed to do.

His mommy would ask him to do his homework from school, and he would say, "I'll do it tomorrow, Mom."

"No, you must do it today because tomorrow will be too late. You will already be in school, and your homework won't be done!"

So, Amos had to do his homework even though he didn't want to.

When his daddy asked him to take out the garbage, Amos would say, "I'll do it tomorrow."

"No, Amos, it has to be taken out today, because tomorrow it won't smell so nice." Amos didn't want to take out the garbage today, but his daddy had asked him to. So, Amos took the garbage bags to the curb so that

the garbage men would be able to pick them up
tomorrow.

Amos' friends asked him to play with them. "I'll do it
tomorrow," Amos said. He had other things that he
would rather do!

Now Amos loved to play football. That was the game
that he loved most of all. He was a really good player!

One day his friends stopped by, and asked him to come
play football with them.

"I can't today, but I will tomorrow," he said.

The next day his friends stopped by, and asked him once
again to come out and play football with them.

What did Amos say to them? Of course he said, "I'll do
it tomorrow."

A short time later, Amos said, "I don't have anything to
do today so I think I will go play football with my
friends." When he got to the vacant field where all of his
friends were, he said, "I've come to play with you today."

His friends said, "No, you can't play with us, we have
already chosen our players, and you didn't come
yesterday, or the day before!"

Amos had to just sit and watch his friends playing, and
they were having so much fun. He wished that he was
playing, too!

Amos' mother's birthday came up, and Amos said, "I'll wish her a happy birthday and give her a big hug, tomorrow." Tomorrow came, and Amos forgot to say "Happy birthday" to his mother, or to give her a big hug!

That night he heard his mommy crying. "What is the matter, Mommy?" he asked. It broke Amos' heart to see his mommy crying!

"Why, yesterday was my birthday, and you didn't wish me a happy birthday, or give me a hug, and that is why I am so sad. I thought that you loved me," said his mother.

"But, I do love you, Mommy." Amos said. "I will always love you, and I never want to see you cry again!"

His mommy said, "Give me a big hug then, if you love me!" Amos gave his mommy the biggest hug she had ever gotten!

From that moment on, Amos never even thought of saying, *I'll do it tomorrow.* All that he thought of right then was, "If I had done this yesterday, my mommy wouldn't be so sad right now!"

So, Amos never, ever said, "I'll do it tomorrow" again!

But, you know you can still say "I'll do it tomorrow." Tell your mommy that you want to give her a big kiss right now, and then tell her "I'll do it tomorrow!"

Good night.

AMOS GIVING MOMMY A BIG HUG

THE LITTLE COUNTRY STORE

On a corner where two busy highways crossed, there stood a little country store. It was a nice little store. It liked everyone. And everyone liked it! It even had a name. Do you want to know its name? It was Horton's Country Store.

From now on, we will call the little country store 'Horton.' Now, when Horton was very young, he had only a few things to sell to the little boys and girls who came in to visit him. But as he got older, he became bigger and bigger until one day he had candy, he had kites, he had cold drinks, and he had everything else boys and girls could want.

Everyone came to visit him, and to see what he had to sell. Horton loved it, because he just loved people. He loved to see little girls play happily with the toys he had to sell. He loved seeing the little boys play with all the things they would need to go fishing. He had corks and bobbers. He had fishing lines. Why, he even had fishing poles and worms to fish with! Everyone was very happy with the way things were!

Then one day a terrible thing happened. A new store

came to the city near where Horton lived. It was a big, big, store! That big store had everything that Horton had, and lots more! It had a nice restaurant. It had a movie theater. It even had a great big toy department!

Every one of Horton's friends decided to go to the big store to see what was there for sale. It surely saddened Horton when his little friends stopped coming in to see him every time they needed something. He missed his friends!

Poor, sad little Horton. But, things weren't going to be this way forever. Now don't go to sleep just yet, and I will tell you what happened. But promise you will go to sleep when we finish this story.

One of Horton's little friends, and her mother, were in the big store getting a Father's day gift for her dear dad. At the checkout counter, the mother saw that she didn't have enough money to pay for the gift.

The mother told the clerk, "Just wrap it for me and I will come back tomorrow and pay for it."

"No, sorry, I can't do that," said the clerk, "You will have to leave the gift, and I will give it back to you tomorrow when you bring me the money!"

"But," the little girl said, "Tomorrow will be too late, because today is Father's Day!"

"Sorry, I can't help you," said that mean-spirited old clerk. So, sadly, they left the big store without a Father's Day gift!

"Mommy," the little girl said on their way home, "Horton would have given the gift to us for daddy."

"I know," said the little girl's mother. "I will do all of my shopping with Horton from now on, because Horton knows me, and he is a much friendlier store. I surely wish that I had gone to see Horton today!"

Another of Horton's friends, and his mom, went to the big, new store to buy some milk, one rainy day.

The milk cooler in the store looked very nice. It had all kinds of milk. It even had chocolate milk to sell! It was a pretty store. Horton's friends paid for the milk, and went to their car to drive home, dodging raindrops the whole way.

The car would not start! "Oh no," cried the little boy's mother, "I will have to go back inside the big store and ask them to call for help!"

The little boy's mother dodged raindrops all the way back into that store, and asked the owner to call for help. The mean old owner said that he did not have the time to call anyone! He did not want to be bothered with her. Finally, she found a telephone and called for help. And she didn't know it, but the man who came to help was one of Horton's friends.

On their way home that day, the little boy said to his mother, "Mommy, Horton would have helped us. He always found the time to help people."

"I know," said the mother, "From now on, we will always go to Horton when we need something."

Time and time again, Horton's friends found out just how badly they needed his little country store! It wasn't like the big, big store, you see. For Horton knew everyone, and he liked everyone. He even knew them well enough that he had their stuff ready for them as soon as he saw them drive up, and even before they could come inside! And, if you didn't have the money right then with you, it was okay to pay him tomorrow!

Sooner or later, all of Horton's friends came back to shop with him. And, as you might imagine, they were very happy to do so. Even today, you can still hear the laughter of the little boys and girls in Horton's store. And if you listen very closely, you can even hear Horton laughing, too!

Good night.

A SHARK NAMED HENRY

You might be wondering why anyone would name a shark Henry? I don't know the answer to that question, either. People think that sharks are mean, so you would think this shark's name would be Tiger, or maybe Hammer, but no... how about Bull? *No, again!* Well, let's just don't worry about what his name is *not*, let's just call him Henry, which is his real name. Maybe the other sharks who named him had a favorite uncle named Henry. How will we ever know?

Henry loved to travel. He swam in all of the oceans on our beautiful earth.. (Do you know how many oceans there are on earth?) That means that Henry had to do a lot of traveling, doesn't it?

Well, everywhere that Henry went, he scared people. Most people are just naturally afraid of sharks. Little boys and girls just did not want to swim with him, because they are afraid of sharks, too. That is actually a good idea, since mother nature doesn't want us to play with sharks. She wants sharks to play with other sharks, not with people!

But Henry was not a bad shark. As a matter of fact, he was a very nice one! He did not ever want to hurt a little girl or boy. So, he thought it would be best if he did not ever try to play with them. He would sit out in the ocean close to the beach, and watch kids playing in the big waves, and making sandcastles on the beach. It was very sad, because he would never even let the kids see him. He sometimes wished that he was a little boy or girl, just so he could play with them, too. But Henry was a shark, and there was nothing he could do about that!

One of his favorite kids was a little girl named Alyssa. She was a very pretty little girl. She had a smile that just lit up her whole face, and always made you want to smile right back at her. All of the other kids loved her, also. Alyssa was so nice that everyone who met her just seemed to fall in love with her.

But one day Alyssa was at the beach playing in the sand, making sandcastles, when she decided to go for a swim. She did something that little kids should never do; she didn't tell her mommy she was going into the water! She did take her life jacket, but she did not put it on the right way.

Alyssa had only gone a short distance out into the water, when a huge wave came towards her. She turned and ran as fast as she could to the shore. But she wasn't fast enough! The big wave caught up with her, and with a loud splash, knocked poor Alyssa to the sea floor. It also knocked that life jacket right off of her

Now Alyssa was in really big trouble, because she couldn't keep her head above the water in order to breathe! She could not call out to her mommy, because every time she opened her mouth, it seemed to fill up with water. What was she going to do? I'll bet you already know!

Now, here comes our hero! I am talking about Henry, of course. He had to be very careful not to let Alyssa see him. She was scared enough, already! Henry grabbed that life jacket, and with a toss of that mighty tail, threw it right into Alyssa's arms! Alyssa finally got the jacket on the right way, and excitedly got back to the sand. She even thought she had felt a little nudge along the way!

Alyssa's mommy never knew what happened that day. Alyssa never really knew what happened that day, either! But, she always wondered how that life jacket just seemed to jump into her hands!

So our hero just swam back into the deepest parts of the ocean, all the while feeling very good about himself. Henry should feel good about his behavior, since Alyssa was not the first child he had saved. He had done this many times before Alyssa, and he saved three more kids after her.

You see, Henry had always been a hero, but no one would ever know!

And just what does this tell us about Henry's behavior…

- **real heroes do the right thing, whether anybody is watching, or not.**
- **real heroes do not brag about the good that they do, they just feel good on the inside, for having helped out.**

Good night.

HENRY THE SHARK HELPS SAVE ALYSSA

RUSTY HELPS HIS FAMILY

I will tell you my name. It is Rusty. But, I won't tell you what I am yet! I'll bet you can guess what I am, after I tell you a few things about myself. Then you can tell me what you think that I am.

In the mean*time*, let's start our story.

I was once a very pretty thing, bright and shiny. I have numbers all around me, and I'm something that someone would wear on their wrist. I have two hands just like you do. Do you have any idea what I am yet? I bet you're getting warm...

I was once used all the *time*, but newer, prettier, machines came along, able to do the same things that I do, and much more. Pretty soon I was tossed onto a shelf. I sat there sad and all alone on that shelf, for a long, long *time*.

I will give you another little hint as to what I am. I have used the word *"TIME"* three *times* already, oops, now, it's four!

I can tell you when to wake up. I can tell you when to go to bed. I can tell you when to eat. I can even tell you when to go to school! Do you know what I am yet? I have to tell you now, so that we can continue with the story.

Have you guessed that I am a *wristwatch?* I love being strapped on, and going to all those places with my master... I really miss being taken along.

Now, my grandfather was a really big clock, who sat in the living room of this huge house. Whenever he wanted to tell everyone the time, he just shouted it out with big *dong, dong, dongs*.

My cousins were all pretty electric clocks, who sat on mantles, and on tables, and everywhere in the kitchen, and in the bedrooms. They were all mean to me, because I was just a wristwatch, and getting very old!

Finally, I sat on that shelf for so long, that I finally got rust all over me. That is why my mean cousins started calling me Rusty! You wouldn't be that mean, would you? I didn't think so!

"Hey, Rusty," one mean cousin called to me once. "Do you think that it is time to put you in the garbage can?"

Rusty could still tell time, and he didn't think that was very funny to say, do you? Well, all of that changed one day! Rusty was sitting on his shelf, wishing that he was still on somebody's wrist, when he heard a very loud noise. Boom! It was thunder! Then the rain came, then the wind started howling. And all of a sudden, it got very dark in the house where Rusty lived. All of the electricity had gone off.

The television set stopped working, the washing machine stopped running. And, do you know what else stopped working? Yes, all the pretty clocks!

Every person in that house was worried because they didn't know what time it was. Everyone had appointments, those special somethings, which they all had to do at certain times during the day. They looked at all of the pretty clocks, but none of them were working. Not one could tell them what time it was. All they could do was blink, saying that it was
12:00... blink...
>*12:00... blink...*
>>*12:00... blink...*
>>>*12:00...*
It was very important that they knew what time it was... but, now how could they?

"I know," said the father of the family. "Where is my old wristwatch? It will always tell us what time it is!"

The pretty new clocks heard that, and boy, did they wish that they had never teased their cousin, the wristwatch!

Well, that father finally found Rusty. He quickly put Rusty on his wrist.

"I don't know why I ever put you on that shelf, anyhow!" the father said. "From now on, you will be on my wrist, for that is where you belong."

Rusty just loved being back on the father's wrist. And it felt just exactly like that is where he would always want to be.

We can't call him Rusty anymore, because he just isn't rusty. He needs a new name. Can you give Rusty a new name? Oh, and by the way, the former Rusty says that it is *time* to go to sleep!

Good night.

MATT BAT

Matt Bat is a bat who lives a long, long way from you and me. He lives in a state called New Mexico. Do you know where New Mexico is? After you finish with this story, go to sleep, and then tomorrow ask your parents if they have a map of the United States, then have someone help you find New Mexico. Do you think that you can find it by yourself?

On with the story! Most people are afraid of bats. Are you afraid of bats? There is no reason to be, since bats are our friends. Yes, that's just what I said, bats are our friends. Do you believe me? Bats are our friends just like the birds, and the animals, and trees and flowers are, too. You see, bats love to eat insects, especially insects that like to bite us. If there were no bats, there would be millions and zillions more biting insects looking for us. Would you agree now that bats are our friends? Well, yes, and that brings us to the very beginning of our story.

Dianne is a human person, just like you and me. She had a problem. She could never go out in her yard to play, because there were so many insects out there that liked to bite her. And that's too bad, because she had so many wonderful toys in her yard to play with.

She had a wagon, she had a swing-set, and Dianne even had a treehouse, up in a tree in her backyard! But, she could never go outside to play with all those toys. You see, insects just loved to nibble on Dianne.

Our buddy Matt Bat lived very close by Dianne's house. She wasn't afraid of Matt. She even thought that he was cute. Matt would watch Dianne when she ran out of the house to get into her daddy's car, and he wondered why she always ran. Also, he wondered why she never came outside to play with all those nice toys?

Can you tell why she always ran to the car? Do you know why she never came outside to play with her toys? Tell me why? You're right…those bugs bite!

Now, Dianne was a nice girl, and she was always doing nice things for her friends. She was always helping someone. Matt liked her, just because she was so nice.

One day a human named James came inside of Matt's cave. Did you know that bats love to live in caves?

James saw Matt, and said "My, what an ugly creature you are!"

Dianne heard James say that, and got really mad!

"They are not ugly," she said. "I think they are beautiful creatures. And, you know, they help humans all the time!"

"I don't care, I still think they are ugly," James said.

Well, old James was about to change his mind about
bats. James had just moved into Dianne's neighborhood,
and he wanted to have a party to invite all of the
neighbors over for a cookout, so he could meet them all.
Now that was a good idea, except for one, teenie-eenie
thing. Do you know what that one, teenie-eenie thing
could be? Did you say insects? I thought you did! They
are teenie-eenie, aren't they?

Dianne wanted James to have the cookout, too. She
loved cookouts, and meeting new people. But, she knew
that they couldn't have one because of the bugs, so she
became very sad!

Matt saw Dianne become sad, so it made him sad, too.
He flew down to Dianne's window, and looked in.

Dianne saw Matt bat and said, "I wish that there were a
lot of good bats like you around here, so you could get rid
of all those mean insects! Just the mean insects," she
said, "there are a lot of good insects, too!"

Dianne didn't know it, but Matt had thousands and
thousands of friends that could help. He went back to his
cave, and told all of his friends about Dianne, and of her
problem. He even went to different caves, far and wide,
caves where millions more bats lived. All of those bats
wanted to help Dianne, because Matt told them that she
had always been their friend.

The night before the cookout, Matt and all of those other bats swooped down on James's yard. In no time at all, they ate all of those bad, stinging insects. James heard the whooshing noise that all of those bats were making with their wings, swooshing in the air. When he looked outside, he couldn't believe it. All of the mean insects were gone!

Now James could have his cookout. And he did! All of the neighbors came, especially after they heard about how all the insects had been gobbled up by the bats. James got to meet all of his new neighbors, and he quickly made friends. He also changed his mind about bats being ugly. Now that he really got to know the bats, he saw that they were not ugly at all, just different from him.

Do you think that Dianne was able to come to James' cookout? Now, you probably think that this is the end of the story, but it's not! We haven't solved Dianne's problem yet, have we? We're not going to, but Matt Bat will.

Matt finally realized why Dianne never came outside to play with all those nice toys . So, do you know what he did? Matt got all of his bat friends to come to Dianne's house every night when she was asleep, and they ate all of those bad insects. He did this forever and ever! He never told Dianne what he did for her, but she knew all along.

Now Matt and Dianne are always smiling. Dianne is smiling because she can play with her toys. Matt is smiling because he sees his friend Dianne smiling. And she never has to run to her car, anymore, either. She can walk to it now. How do you feel about bats now? Do you like bats now? Close your eyes, and try to picture all those whirring, stirring bat wings, swooping through those bad, biting bugs… can you see them cleaning out Dianne's yard?

Good night.

| DIANNE IS WATCHING MATT BAT EAT THE INSECTS |

BARTRAM, THE MANATEE WHO JUST WANTED TO HELP

Do any of you kids know what a manatee is? Do you know? What is another name for a manatee? Is it a sea cow? You said sea cow before I did, didn't you? I knew that you knew that other name all along.

This story is about a manatee named Bartram. He was a great, big old manatee. But, did you know that all manatees are big? And they just love to hang around places that you and I also like; places like big rivers and tributaries. Boy, tributary is a big word, isn't it? Do you know what a tributary is? Tell me what you think a tributary is?

Bartram loved this one pond that was close to a big river. The pond was full of things that Bartram loved to eat. It was Bartram's home. He had everything that he needed right there. It had lots and lots of green plants, and manatees love green plants. Yes sir, Bartram ate his vegetables every single day. Do you?

Now, on the shore of that big pond lived a man and his wife. His name was Bill and his wife's name was Ann. Bill and Ann didn't like manatees. They liked to get into their boat and just fish all over that pond. Sometimes they would be in a hurry, and want to go real fast in their boat, but they couldn't do that, because they might hurt the manatees. Bill and Ann didn't care for manatees, but they didn't want to hurt them, either.

**BARTRAM THE HELPFUL MANATEE
ENJOYING HIS FAVORITE POND**

One day Bartram was just lying about enjoying the warm summer sun, when Bill and Ann came floating by in their boat.

He heard Bill say, "I wish that manatee would move somewhere else. He is in my way all the time!"

That comment really hurt Bartrams feelings. He felt so sad! *I don't want to stay in a place where the people don't like me, so I will move*, Bartram thought.

So off he went looking for a new home. He knew that he would never find one that he liked as much as that last one. But he finally found a shabby little pond that wasn't very pretty, and decided to live there. He knew that he would never be as happy there, though, but he would try.

Bill and Ann saw Bartram moving, and they were really happy. But they were going to be happy only for a little while. They didn't know what was about to happen. With Bartram gone, the pond started getting thicker and thicker with those green plants, until one day it was so thick that Bill couldn't get his boat through. Now Bill and Ann had a problem. They loved to fish. They loved to ride in their boat. They loved to just float around the pond on a nice sunny day. Now they could not do any of these things, because of the green plants. And do you know what would have kept those plants from getting so big? I forgot, so will you tell me? I was just kidding! Bill and Ann really needed Bartram back to eat those plants.

"I wish that big old manatee was back here," Bill said to Ann. *Me too,* Ann thought.

Well, there just happened to be a great big bullfrog sitting on a lilly pad close to where Bill and Ann were, and he heard everything that they said. He also knew Bartram, and how sad he was about not living in that nice pond anymore. So he hip-hopped all over the place looking for Bartram, and he finally found him. Poor Bartram had a very sad look on his face. He wasn't happy in that new, little pond. But that bullfrog was about to change all of that.

When Bartram found out that Bill and Ann wanted him back to that nice pond, he didn't even take the time to pack his clothes. Wait a minute! Manatees don't wear clothes, anyhow! Well, he didn't take the time to pack anything! He just swam as fast as any manatee could, which is real pokey, back to that old, favorite pond.

Bill and Ann saw Bartram coming, and went out by the edge of the pond to greet him.

"I am sorry I said those things about you," Bill said. "If you will stay here, I will be the best friend you will ever have!"

In just a few days, Bartram had eaten so many of those green veggies that the pond was looking as good as new. Bill and Ann could get in their boat and fish, and just float around on those warm sunny days. Bill was happy! Ann was happy! The bullfrog was happy! But do you know who was the happiest? Tell me, I forgot again!

Good night.

Bob Morgan

BOBBY BOBBY WITH A HOBBY

In a big city, in a big country, on the other side of a big ocean, lives a policeman named Bobby. The name of the big city that Bobby lives in is London. The name of the country that London is in, is England. The name of the ocean is the Atlantic. And in London, the policemen are called bobbies. So, that is why we call him Bobby bobby. Can you find London, England on a map?

Now, Bobby bobby had a hobby. He loved to get his camera out and take pictures. He would take pictures of cows and horses. He would take pictures of trees and birds. He even took a picture of a tadpole once. But most of all, he loved to take pictures of beautiful flowers.

In London, very close to where Bobby worked when he was on duty as a bobby, there lived a little old lady. Her name was Mrs. Crobby. She just loved beautiful flowers. She loved to smell the flowers. She loved to look at the flowers. She loved to touch them, too. She would spend all day in her garden taking care of them. She made sure that her flowers had lots of water to drink. She made sure that her flowers had everything they needed to stay beautiful.

But, as the years passed by, Mrs. Crobby got older and older, until finally she was just too old to care for her flowers anymore! Also, she had no one to take care of her flowers for her. As wintertime approached, old Jack Frost came and froze up all of Mrs. Crobby's flowers. She looked out of her window, and was really sad to see that her pretty flowers were all gone. Which, of course, made Mrs. Crobby really sobby!

Now, Bobby bobby heard that Mrs. Crobby was very sobby! And he knew exactly what to do about it! Next spring, when it was nice and warm again, he would plant brand new flowers for Mrs. Crobby. Bobby bobby, as you know, was a very nice bobby, and he had quite a hobby! What was Bobby bobby's hobby?

Springtime finally came. The days were nice and warm. The birds came back and started singing again. The cows came out of the barns. The horses came out of the stables. Everyone and everything seemed to come out and enjoy the beautiful days. And Bobby bobby had a job to do.

Bobby bobby went to Mrs. Crobby's garden, and replanted all her flowers. He planted really pretty ones, too. He planted the kind that he knew Mrs. Crobby loved the most. And he planted them right by Mrs. Crobby's window, so she could see them all day long.

When the flowers grew up and started blooming, it sure was a sight to see. The bees loved those flowers, the hummingbirds loved them, and if you would be very still, you would even see butterflies fluttering all around them, too. But most of all, Mrs. Crobby loved them. She thought that Bobby's flowers were even more beautiful than the ones she used to plant.

But wintertime was going to come again. Bobby bobby knew this, and he was going to do something about it this time. When the flowers were at their most beautiful, Bobby bobby used his hobby to help Mrs. Crobby, so she wouldn't become sobby again. He took pictures of the flowers. Really nice pictures, beautiful, big pictures. They were just as pretty as the real flowers.

Wintertime did come again, and sure enough, old Jack Frost came to visit once more. Mrs. Crobby was so sad to see the frost come, because she knew that her flowers would be gone again. And sure enough, in no time at all, the pretty flowers were gone. Poor old Mrs. Crobby!

But our friend Bobby bobby, with the hobby, went to see the sobby Mrs. Crobby. He brought all the pictures of those pretty flowers with him. One by one, he put them up, all around Mrs. Crobby's home, until each room had a picture of beautiful flowers in it.

Mrs. Crobby said to Bobby bobby, "They look so real, even more real than when they were in my garden. And I can get so close to them, and I can touch them. Why, I can almost smell them! Thank you Bobby, you have made an old lady very happy."

It made Bobby bobby very happy, too. He just loved helping people. And next spring, he would plant even more flowers for Mrs. Crobby.

After all, Bobby bobby didn't want to see another sobby Mrs. Crobby! He wanted her to stay happy, and she was happy now.

Good night.

BILLY BOAT
AND THE BILLY GOAT

On a seashore, near a lighthouse, far, far away, lived a boat named Billy. Billy Boat was a nice little boat. He had a very pretty sail. The top part of his sail was red. The middle part of his sail was white. And the bottom part of his colorful sail was blue. Billy loved to sail around on the cool blue, ocean water.

On that same seashore, by that same lighthouse, there lived a goat named Billy. Billy Goat wasn't a very happy little goat, for you see, all of his friends lived on an island a long way from the seashore. Billy Goat could look over and see his friends playing on that island all the time, and all that he could think about was to somehow, someday find a way to get to that island! But it was just too far to try to swim there. How would Billy Goat get to that island? Will he ever find a way? What do you think?

One clear summer day, Billy Boat was sailing on the cool water all by himself, having a good time, when it happened! Billy Boat's bottom hit a big rock, and that mean, sharp old rock put a big hole right in Billy Boat's bottom.

"Oh, no," he cried! "What am I going to do?"

Just as fast as his sail could push him, Billy Boat ran towards the shore where shallow water and soft sand made it safe. If he had not done that, Billy boat would have sunk to the bottom of the sea, and no one would have ever found him! Billy Boat made it to the seashore that day, thanks to his friend, the wind.

But, once he got there, what was he to do? He couldn't repair himself. He needed help! And there was no help to be found. Or, was there?

Billy Boat sat there on that seashore for a long time, thinking that there was never going to be any help for him. He was scared! He was sad. He tried to be a big boy, but one night he started crying. It was okay for him to cry. We all cry sometimes.

Billy Goat was on that same seashore, that same night, and he was crying, too. He was so very lonely. He wanted to be with his friends. After he dried his eyes, he heard something strange. It was Billy Boat crying, and he sounded so sad!

Billy Goat went over to Billy Boat and asked him, "What is wrong?"

Billy Boat said to Billy Goat, "I am broken and have no one to repair me! I guess that I will have to stay here forever!"

"No, you won't," Billy goat said, "I know how to repair you, so just sit still and I will have you fixed up in no time at all."

So Billy Goat started hammering and nailing and gluing. By morning, Billy Boat was as good as new! He was better than before, because he had a new coat of paint on, too!

So, Billy Goat pushed Billy Boat back into the water. Boy, did that ever feel good to Billy Boat! He slowly raised that pretty sail, and he was once again sailing smoothly on the water, doing what he loved to do. He looked back at Billy Goat to wave goodbye, and he noticed that sad look on Billy Goat's face.

"What is wrong, Billy Goat, I thought that you would be happy this morning."

"I was happy to help you, Billy Boat, but I miss my friends on that island, and I can't swim far enough to ever get to see them, or to play with them!"

Billy Boat turned himself around, went back to the seashore, and told Billy Goat, "Why didn't you tell me last night? We can fix that problem right away! Jump on, and I will have you there before you can count to ten."

So, Billy Goat jumped onto Billy Boat, and sure enough, before Billy Goat could count to ten, he was on that island with his friends. They were all so glad to see him, and

they said they all wanted to play with him, too. Billy Goat was so happy!

BILLY GOAT RIDING IN BILLY BOAT

Bob Morgan

"I will come pick you up tonight and take you back home, Billy Goat," Billy Boat said. And he did! Forever and ever!

Billy Goat thought to himself, *I did just one little kind thing and look at how much happiness it brought me!*

And Billy Boat thought to himself, *I did just one kind little thing and look at all the happiness it brought me!*

Good night.

BECKY, THE HARDWORKING LITTLE COMPUTER

In a big office building, in a big city, there was a little computer named Becky. Now, Becky had been around that office building for a very, very long time. She knew everything there was to know about how to run an office. Whenever someone asked Becky a question, they just knew that she was going to give them the right answer. She was always there at work, and was always handy to have around.

There were a lot of people working in that office, all of them counting on Becky to answer their questions. And Becky always did! One of the people was named Madeline. She asked Luis, another person in Becky's office, how to spell a big word.

Luis said, "Wow, that is a big word, and I don't know how to spell it! Ask Becky!"

Well, Madeline asked Becky how to spell that big word and Becky, without even thinking, gave Madeline the answer.

"Thank you Becky," Madeline said.

Eileen and Myrtle were trying to add some big numbers together one day, and could not get the right answer. Do you know what they did? Of course, they asked Becky! And Becky gave them the right answer!

Steve and Rebecca were trying to find out where a country was on the map, but they just could not find out where the little country was. It was so small, that even the maps did not know where it was, so what did they do? They asked Becky! Do you think Becky told them where the little country was? Sure, she did!

Carolyn and Marylou wanted to know where the White House was. Do you know who lives in the White House? Do you know where the White House is? Becky told them.

Then one day, a terrible thing happened. The person who was the office boss came into the office, and told everyone, "Today we are all getting new computers. Becky is getting older and we need new ones."

"Oh no," cried Becky, what will they do with me? I hope they don't throw me away!"

So, later on that day, all of the people in that office had brand new shiny computers, but they wanted to keep Becky, since they loved her so. She had been a good friend for a long, long time. So, off to the shelf in the back room went Becky. She was so sad, she felt like crying, and she did. No one wanted her anymore. Or did they?

Peggy and Barbara were working on a big problem the very next day. They wanted to send some messages to another office, on the other side of the city. But the new computers were young, and had not learned everything yet, and could not help them.

Becky would have known and she would have been happy to help us, they thought to themselves.

One day, Susan and Doris were trying to find out who had been the first President of the United States. Do you know who the first President was? Okay then, who is the President right now? The new computer wasn't working that day.

Everyone in that office thought the very same thing. *Let's get Becky out here, and off of that shelf in the back room. We need her here!*

So, all of the people in that office started clearing a spot for Becky. And do you know where they put her? Right in the middle of that big, old office. Now, everyone could get all of their questions answered once again. They were all happy. The boss was happy. But do you know who was the happiest of all? Tell me!

Good night.

Bob Morgan

**GOOD OLD BECKY THE COMPUTER,
IN THE MIDDLE OF THE OFFICE, BACK ON THE JOB!**

I LOVE LIVING IN A TREE

When I was first born, it was in the springtime. I didn't know what I was. I was a little red thing on a tree branch. I wondered, *What am I? Do you remember seeing me?*

Then, as I got a little older, I turned bright green. I loved that color. I was shiny, and much bigger, then. I lived up in the very tip-top of a big tree.

One day, a squirrel and his family built a big squirrel's nest right there beside me. It was truly lots of fun watching those squirrels scampering back and forth, the way they do. They were gathering nuts for the winter, which would surely be coming.

I didn't know anything about winter way back then. The squirrels would go out each morning, and gather their nuts. Sometimes when they would find more nuts than they could carry, they would stuff some into their cheeks for safe keeping. Which, by the way, was another funny thing to see.

The little baby squirrel would try to carry as many nuts as his parents, but he couldn't get his little mouth to open wide enough. So, he would only carry one nut at a time, but he was trying very hard!

One day I heard the squirrels talking. The father squirrel said to the mother squirrel, "Well, winter is almost here, and I do believe we are ready. We finally have our nest completely full of nuts. We will know when wintertime comes, because when it does, that leaf over there will change colors."

When the father squirrel said the word, "...leaf over there...", he was pointing right, directly at me. So, I thought, *that's what I am, I'm a leaf. Did you see me when I was bright, and shiny, and green?*

One day, another family came to visit me. It was a family of bluebirds. They built a nest just beneath me. They were lots of fun to watch, also. I watched as the father and mother bluebird brought twigs, one at a time, and slowly wove that nest. With both of them working together, it didn't take very long. It was a very nice nest. I enjoyed listening to those bluebirds fill the treetops with their songs. I would sway back and forth with the breeze when they sang. The breeze seemed to love their songs, too.

The hot summer had come, stayed, and was leaving now. It was getting cooler and cooler each morning. Then, one morning, it was really cold. I didn't know what was happening.

I watched, as the squirrel and his family crawled into their nest as if they were never coming out again!

I saw the bluebird and his family leaving their home, as if they were never coming back. What is wrong? Are they mad at me? I hope that they are not all mad at me!

I didn't know it at the time, but the squirrels were settling in for the cold weather that was coming soon. I also didn't know that the bluebirds were traveling further south, where it is much warmer during the winter. Sadly, now I am here, all alone.

I woke up one morning, and lo and behold, the ground was very white. Nothing looked right to me. It was frost. Oh yes, old Jack Frost!

Old Jack Frost said to me, "Don't be afraid, I am here because Mother Nature sent me. I come every year. I do a lot of good things while I am here. Do you remember last spring when you were just a little red thing on a tree branch? Well, I am the one that helped you become that little red thing. You won't be able to remember it, but I was here the year before that, and the year before that! And I will be here every year, forever and ever! And I will help you each time I come!"

Now, for some reason, I am not afraid anymore. I would like to be a little red thing on a tree branch again. I would like to become a big green leaf, and watch the squirrels and the birds build nests next to me again, which they will surely do.

I am turning brown now. I feel myself letting go of the tree that I called home for so long. The tree seems sad that I am leaving, too. But don't worry, tree, for I will come back in the spring, and I will help you be pretty once again.

Now, don't you children feel sad for me, either. For I will be back in the spring, I promise. Do you promise to look for me?

Good night.

THE FAMILY THAT BUILT
A REALLY, REALLY BIG TREEHOUSE

I am going to begin this story with "Once Upon A Time…" Do you think that I should? Okay, here goes!

Once upon a time, there was a group of friends who wanted a treehouse. That is all they ever wanted. They thought about it all the time. They wanted to use it for a clubhouse, but none of them knew how to build a treehouse.

Another group of kids, on the other side of town, had a treehouse. So, one day they all walked over to the other side of town, to look the other kids' treehouse. It was a small treehouse. It had no windows, and it had no doors. It was made of a rough wood, which was not very pretty. But, it certainly was a treehouse!

They asked the other kids if they could come up, and play in the treehouse with them.

"No," they said, "You can't come up and play in our treehouse. Go build your own!" They were some pretty mean kids, don't you think? You would share your treehouse, wouldn't you? I thought so!

Well, the kids who always wanted a treehouse were named Jamie, Sarah, and Katy. They didn't know what they were going to do, for they certainly didn't know how to even begin building a treehouse. Yet they wanted one so much.

Early that day, Jamie, Sarah, and Katy were so sad that tears were beginning to show up. Yes, they were that sad. Just when they thought that they would never get a treehouse started, something wonderful happened.

Their father, Keith, just happened to love working with wood, and he could build just about anything. When he found out why they were so sad, he said "I'll bet I can make all of you happy again! I know how to build a treehouse, and I will build one just for you girls. This will be the biggest, prettiest treehouse that you have ever seen. And, I will ask your mother if she will help, too."

Now, Tammy, their mom, was the right person to ask for help. She was always helping someone. Whenever anybody needed anything, Tammy would be the first one there to help. Keith and Tammy were very nice people.

Keith went right to work on that treehouse. Soon a floor was taking shape. Then, the walls seemed to suddenly spring up in the branches. And not too long after that, why, the roof was on! And that treehouse was getting to be very big. It was almost as big as the house that Tammy, Keith, Jamie, Sarah, and Katy lived in. But, there seemed to be something missing.

What else does it need? Keith thought to himself. *I know what it needs, a nice coat of paint.*

After Keith finished painting the treehouse, Tammy looked at it and thought, *it still needs something. Let me think... aha, I know what it needs. It needs curtains over the windows. It needs a nice welcome mat. It needs beautiful lights, too!* When Tammy finished with that treehouse, it was absolutely beautiful! It was just as pretty as the house that their whole family lived in.

Those three kids gave their father and their mother big hugs and kisses, for building that treehouse for them. Now they had the nicest treehouse in the town. They had the nicest treehouse that anybody had ever even seen. Of course they started playing in it right away!

The mean old kids from the other side of town heard about that treehouse, and they came over to see it.

Wow, they thought, *what a treehouse!* "Can we come up and play in it?"

What would you do? Would you let them come up? If you didn't let them come up and play, wouldn't that make you just as mean as they were? And you don't ever want to be that mean, do you?

Well, that big old treehouse was certainly large enough to hold all of those kids, and even more than that. After awhile, it was the place where all of the kids met and played, and they all loved it.

Tammy and Keith loved it too, because it made a lot of kids very happy! I'm pretty sure that the treehouse was happy, too!

Good night from the treehouse kids.

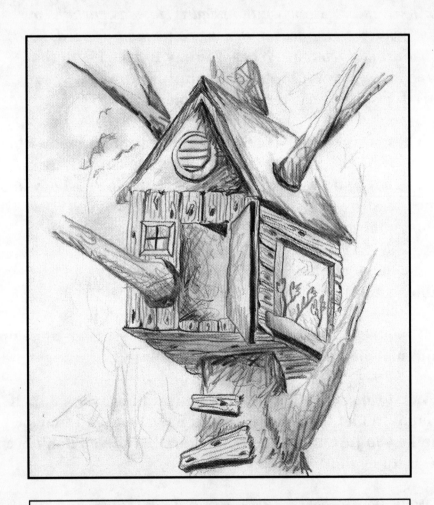

THE REALLY, REALLY BIG TREEHOUSE

TUMBLES, THE TUMBLING WEED, AND THE WIND

In a place far, far away, there lives a weed named Tumbles. Tumbles is a tumbling tumbleweed. Do you know where tumbleweeds live? Tomorrow morning, look on a map of the American Southwest. When you find it, show your parents where Tumbles lives. Promise Tumbles that you will find out where he lives.

Old Tumbles likes to travel, but the only way that he can move is by the blowing of the wind. He has no arms or legs, like you or me. He's shaped just like a round ball. That is why the wind can move him so easily. So, every time Tumbles wants to go somewhere, he has to call on his friend, Mr. Wind, to come take him. Mr. Wind likes to help out old Tumbles whenever he can.

One day Tumbles decided that he wanted to go see a big mountain. He had never seen a mountain before. Have you?

"Hey, Mister Wind," Tumbles shouted, "Please take me to see a mountain."

"I'll be happy to take you to a mountain," Mr. Wind said, "I love helping out my good friends."

So Mr. Wind started blowing up a little breeze, then he blew faster and faster. "Is this fast enough, Tumbles?"

"No," said Tumbles, "Let's go lots faster!"

Mr. Wind smiled, and really started howling then. "Is this fast enough, Tumbles?"

"*Wheeee*, this is fun," said Tumbles as he tumbled across the land like a streak. Tumbles sure likes to go fast, doesn't he?

"Are we getting close to the mountain yet, Mr. Wind?"

"Not yet," Mr. Wind said, "But it won't be much longer now." Tumbles couldn't wait to see that mountain!

After they had zipped by a jackrabbit, a roadrunner, and a coyote, Mr. Wind shouted to Tumbles, "Look straight in front of you, Tumbles. Do you see that huge thing sticking up into the clouds? That is the mountain. We are still far away from it, but it is so big that you can even see it now!"

As they got closer and closer, Tumbles could not believe how big the mountain was growing. Finally, they reached the mountain. It was huge! It was so massive, that Tumbles could not see the top anymore.

"Do you want to go all the way to the top, Tumbles?"

"Yes, please Mr. Wind, let's go all the way to the top of this mountain."

So Mr. Wind had to howl up a storm with all of his might, to push Tumbles to the top. Finally, after huffing and puffing for a long time, there sat Mr. Wind and Tumbles on the top of that mountain.

"What a pretty sight to see," said Tumbles.

Everything was so clean and beautiful up there. Tumbles even saw Mr. Eagle flying way down below him, where everything seemed so far away, and so tiny. Why, Tumbles thought that he could even see his own home from way up there on top of that mountain.

"Tumbles, it's time to go back home now," Mr. Wind said.

"Do you think that we can come visit this mountain again someday, Mr. Wind?"

Old Mr. Wind just smiled and said, "Don't you worry, I will bring you back again someday, Tumbles."

So off they went, on their way home. Tumbles looked back at that mountain, and he thought about how beautiful it all was.

"Yes, Mr. Mountain, I would love to come see you again," he said.

When Mr. Wind and Tumbles got home, they were tired, and tumbles was a bit dizzy from tumbling head over heels, over and over, for so long... so off to bed they went.

Again, Tumbles thought about that mountain, and how beautiful it was. Then he thought about his friend, Mr. Wind, for Mr. Wind had helped him all day long, and he never asked for anything in return.

What a good friend Mr. Wind is, Tumbles thought. *You know, his friendship is as big and as beautiful as that mountain. I think that tomorrow I will do something nice for him.*

Good night.

J, THE FRIENDLY FIREMAN

No one knows where he got that name from. His mother didn't even remember why she named him that. But, all of his life, he was known simply as "J". Sometimes it was a problem, because when someone asked him what his name was, he would say "J." They would ask him to spell it, and of course, he would say "J."

When J was a young man, he saw a fireman one day standing on his fire truck, rushing to a fire. The fire truck was painted a very bright red, and it sure was pretty. The fireman went to a house that was burning on J's street, and put out the fire in just no time at all. That fireman wasn't afraid of anything! And J wanted to be just like him!

J studied, and studied everything he could find on how to be a good fireman. He read each book more than once, just to be sure that he didn't miss anything the first time around. J studied really hard in school to make sure that his grades were good enough to pass any test that he might have to take, when he would try to become a fireman.

Finally, the day came when J went to the fire station, to

talk to the Fire Chief about becoming a fireman. He was really excited! He had always wanted to be a fireman.

The Fire Chief looked at all of his test grades, from all the tests that J took all through school. When the Chief finished checking J's grades, he looked up at J and said, "I can tell by all of the studying you did, and by all these good grades you received, that you will be a great fireman."

J was very happy. J was now becoming a fireman. J could now ride on that beautiful, red fire truck. J could now help people, as he always wanted to. And do you know, someday J would become a Fire Chief, too?

J reported to the fire station on his first day. He was even early for work because he was so excited. The Fire Chief gave him a blue uniform to wear. J really looked nice in that uniform, and was he ever proud to wear it!

Then the telephone rang. There was a fire in a small house over on the other side of town. J knew what to do, because he had studied so hard. He threw on that fireman's fire fighting suit, and was in the fire truck, and on his way in no time at all!

When J got to the fire, a little boy grabbed him and said, "My little puppy is still in the house! Please save him!"

J ran into that house and heard the little puppy whimpering, and found him hiding behind the couch.

"Come here, little fella," J said gently, "Let's get you out of here!"

When J came out of the burning house with the little puppy in his arms, all of the neighbors started clapping their hands and calling J a hero. Now, J didn't think that he was a hero! It even embarrassed him just a little bit. He was just doing what any good fireman would have done, he thought. But he did feel pretty good about the job that he did, especially putting out that fire quickly.

After J had been working at the fire station for a few years, all of people came to know him. They liked him very much, because he was so friendly. He had a smile that just made you want to like him. And J was friends with all of the kids in the neighborhood.

One peaceful day, J was at the fire station washing the fire truck. He liked to keep it nice and shiny. He cleaned it so much that most people thought that it sparkled.

Then that telephone rang! It was the telephone that rings only when something bad is happening. J didn't like to hear that one phone ring, because it meant only one thing. Someone is in trouble!

It was a woods fire that was burning just outside of town. Now, J didn't usually fight woods fires, because that is another kind of fire fighter's job. But, there was a little boy playing in those woods, and no one could find him. Everyone knew that if anyone could find that little boy, it would be J!

The other firemen were working really hard to put out that fire, while J went into the woods looking for the little boy. J looked and looked but could not find him. He looked all day and even into the night. He would not give up!

Finally, he heard the little boy crying for help. J rushed over to him and picked him up. "Are you alright?" J asked.

"Yes, I am," the little boy said. "Please show me how to get home."

"I will do even better than that," J said. "I will carry you home."

When J came walking out of the woods with that little boy safely in his arms, all of the people had tears in their eyes. They were so happy. The little boy's parents just wanted to hug the little boy, and J, forever!

Not long after that, J got a letter from a fire station in a big city, a long way from his town. They wanted him to come be their Fire Chief. It was something that J had always wanted. He took that Fire Chief's job, and sadly, moved away.

J visits the old home town every chance he gets, and he is always greeted with a hero's welcome. He misses all of his old friends, but do you know what? He has made new friends in the new city, just the same way he made friends in his hometown; by putting on that wonderful smile, and by being just the same friendly person that he always was!

Every once in a while, the people in J's old hometown

see something in their newspaper about the nice, good things that J has done in that big city.

The newspapers always call him a hero. But J still smiles when he sees that, and thinks to himself, "I am not a hero, I am a fireman, just doing the job that I love."

Good night.

J, THE FRIENDLY FIREMAN

JULIUS, THE GENIUS

Have you ever seen a man who knew just about everything? There was a man who lived very close to you and me, who was just that way. You could ask him any question, and he would know the answer. Do you know the answer to everything? I certainly don't!

This man's name was Julius. He was a big man. He was a very tall man. He was a very handsome man. He loved to laugh. He loved to play all kinds of sports. He loved golf. He loved football. He loved basketball. He loved swimming. He loved skating. He loved fishing. And, as I said, Julius was very smart.

Julius had a wife. Her name was Elizabeth. She didn't love sports the way Julius did, but she loved other things. She loved to cook. She loved to shop. She loved to take care of her kids.

Julius and Elizabeth had three kids, all girls. Their names were Morgan, Bragan, and Aeron. Those three girls all thought that they would never be as smart as their daddy. They were wrong! When they were about the same age as you are, it seemed like to them that their daddy was a genius. He could answer each and every question they asked.

When Julius was at work, all of the people that he worked with would ask him questions. Of course, Julius always had the right answer. They would be just amazed at the knowledge he had. It didn't matter what the question was about, Julius knew the answer! He was a very smart man!

"Daddy, how did you get to be so smart?" Bragan asked her daddy one day, after she saw him helping a friend with an arithmetic problem. (Do you know what "arithmetic" means?)

Julius answered Bragan with a smile, "Everything that I know, I read in books. That is how I got to be smart." So, Bragan started reading every book that she could get her hands on!

"Daddy, how did you get to be so smart?" Aeron asked Julius one time, after a man who worked with Julius asked about how to spell some big word.

"Everything that I know, I learned from a book," Julius said with that same smile. So Aeron started reading everything she could find to read!

"Daddy, how did you get to be so smart?" Morgan asked her daddy one day, as she heard him answer a man's question about who won the football game last week.

"I learned that from reading, too," Julius said, still smiling. "Everything that I know about golf, I learned from reading."

"Everything that I know about football, I learned from reading."

"Everything that I know about basketball, I learned from reading."

"Everything that I know anything about, I learned from reading!"

So Morgan started reading everything. She even borrowed books from her friends! She found a really nice place to borrow books to read, and it was free! Can you tell me what kind of a place Morgan found? There are thousands and thousands of books there to read. Do you know where that place is? It is called a library!

Do you like horses?
Do you like dogs?
Do you like cats?
Do you like giraffes?

No matter what subject you like, you can find a book written about it. And, if you read those books, someday you will be as smart as Julius.

Bragan, Aeron, and Morgan are!

Good night.

I SEE YOU

Do you ever look up into the sky at night? Do you ever look up into the sky when it is very, very dark? Do you see all of those little things twinkling? Do you know what they are called? Yes, you are right, they are called stars!

Well, I am a star. My name is Sammy Star. I was born a very long time ago, and I live very, very far away. It gets lonely up here sometimes. It is when I get lonely that I wish I was a little person, just like you. I watch you playing with all of your friends, and I wish I had someone to play with, too.

I see you even in the daytime, when you can't see me. I see you going to school. I wish I could go to school. I want to learn all of the things that you learn in school.

I see you when your mommy gives you a hug. I wish I had a mommy to hug me. I would love to give her a hug back. I will never know a mommy or a daddy.

I see you when you are in your yard, playing on your swing. I wish I had a swing to play on. I could swing from star to star, and hug all of the other stars that are up here with me.

I see you when you go shopping with your uncle. I wish that I had an uncle to take me shopping. I can't even go shopping by myself. For I am a star, and stars can't shop. I have to stay up here, where I am.

I see you when you go to the park. I wish that I could go to the park and play on the sliding board. I would love to have a picnic on the picnic tables. That looks like so much fun. But, I can't!

But wait, you can't see all of the things that I can see. I can see all of the earth's oceans. They are so beautiful to look at them from up here. The water looks blue, like you have colored it with a soft color crayon. Who colored the oceans? Did you?

I see all of the mountains on earth. Did you color them, too? They are green, and they look like they are trying to reach up to me to just say "hello." They are very pretty. I like to look at the mountains.

I see all of the animals on earth. I love to watch the animals. They are fun to watch. Do you get to see animals? Do you like animals? What is your favorite animal? I love them all!

The whole earth is such a beautiful thing to see. I wish that you could see it the way I do. For I can see the whole world at the same time... It looks like a round, blue ball from here. Did you know that the earth was round?

I love to watch the snow on the mountaintops as it all starts to melt. It makes little marshmallow colored streams, each finding its own way, then joining up to become a big river. Finally, the big rivers flow down, and into the oceans, which all join together. I love to watch the rivers flowing slowly to the oceans.

Now that I think about it, I don't think that I would want to trade places with you, or with anybody. I love it up here too much.

The next time you go outside on a very dark night, look up into the sky and look for me. My name is Sammy Star, and I will see you, and I promise that I will wink at you.

Will you smile and wink back at me?

Good night.

UNCLES AND ANTS

Have you ever tried to have a wonderful picnic, on a very nice day in a beautiful park? Have you ever had a picnic when there were not ants visiting? I think that ants like picnics, too! I *know* that ants like picnics, too!

This is a story about a family of ants who live near a big, wooden picnic table, in a city park near where you and I live. Allow me to introduce you all to this family of ants... here we have the father ant, *Ant*hony; the mother ant, *Ant*oinette; the brother ant, *Ant*werp; and sister ant, *Ant*oole. Then, of course, there are Uncle Ants, and Aunt Ants, aunt *Ant*tillie being the favorite aunt! Ant families are very large, aren't they?

One pretty summer day, all the flowers were in full bloom, the trees were full of rich, green leaves, and the grass felt so good under your feet, that you just needed to take your shoes off. Our friends, the ant family saw a people family, getting ready to have a picnic on that picnic table, right by their home. Just as soon as those people had their wonderful smelling food set out on that wooden table, the ant family came by to visit.

"Shoo, shoo," said the people family to the ant family!

"Go have your own picnic, but leave ours alone!"

This was not the first time that our ant family was asked to leave a people picnic. It happened to them every time! So, the ant family had to leave the people picnic, and go back to the anthill they called home. They were quite sad, since nobody ever made them feel welcome at one of their people picnics.

"I know," said *Ant*hony Ant, "We can have a picnic of our own!"

*Ant*oinette ant added, "I will make the potato salad."

*Ant*werp said, "I will make the baked beans."

"I will bring along the potato chips," said *Ant*oole.

Aunt *Ant*tillie cried out, "and I will bring along paper plates!"

PAPER PLATES!

I didn't know that ants used plates at all, did you? Well, this is going to be some nice picnic, and if that ant family wants to use paper plates, I suppose it will be okay.

Aunt *Ant*tillie said, "I'll go tell all of the rest of the family to come to our picnic." She was the most generous aunt ant.

The big day finally arrived for the great ant picnic. All of the ant family came. It was a sparkling great day for a picnic. The sun was shining, the sky was a deep, rich blue, and even the birds in the trees seemed to be singing this special song... "It's a beautiful day to have a picnic."

And, best of all, there were no people at that picnic table to spoil their picnic. The ants put all of their food on the table, and pretty soon everyone was having the best picnic, EVER!

When the ant picnic was over, all the ants were so happy with the results, that they decided to do this all of the time. And don't you know, they did.

Next time that you go to the park to have a nice picnic with your family, do you think that the ants will bother you? After all, they know how to have their own picnics now.

Of course, they will bother you, because ants just love picnics... theirs, yours, and everyone else's!

Now, close your eyes and dream about your favorite foods at a picnic, and which games you love to play.

Good night.

**UNCLES AND ANTS ON THE PICNIC TABLE
ANTS JUST LOVE PICNICS...
THEIRS, YOURS AND EVERYONE ELSE'S!**

THE ARMADILLO
AND THE COWBOY

Have you ever heard of an armadillo wearing a cowboy hat? I hadn't either, until just the other day. I was talking to an old cowboy friend of mine, when I mentioned an armadillo that ran across the road in front of us.

I said to my friend, "You know, I have seen armadillos all of my life, and I have never seen one do anything good!"

Now, my old cowboy friend stopped me in the middle of my sentence. He was getting really upset at me for saying that.

"I knew of an armadillo that did a lot of good," he said gently. "Sit back, and I'll tell you all about him!"

So, I leaned back against the seat, and wondered what the old cowboy was going to tell me. I really wanted to hear his story, because I didn't believe that an armadillo could ever do a lick of good.

The old timer started out by saying:

"A long time ago in the south, there once lived an armadillo. And, as you know, all armadillos ever do is dig holes. They dig holes in your yard. They dig holes in your driveway. They even dig holes in your flower garden.

Well, it seems like there was this little old lady who had herself a beautiful flower garden. And guess who came to visit? That's right, the armadillo I'm thinking of. And he dug holes all over that garden. Yep, he ruined her flowers. But she caught him. And she told him to leave, and to never come back!

Let's see now, what was his name? Oh yes, that's right, it was Albert. Albert, the armadillo.

Poor Albert really felt bad about tearing up that little old lady's flower garden. So he left, and he never came back. He walked and walked, and then he walked some more. One day he noticed that he had traveled a very long way. Now, he was in a place where there were cows and horses and sheep. Yep, he had walked all the way to Texas!

Just as he was walking over the next big hill, he saw a young cowboy with a horse standing beside him. The cowboy was mending a fence.

"Oh no, the cowboy cried. I have to mend this fence before dark, or all of my cattle will get out, and I have no way to dig holes to put in new fence posts!"

What do you suppose happened then? Of course, Albert ran over to help, because if there is one thing that an armadillo can do, it's dig holes. In hardly no time at all, Albert had a nice fencepost hole dug for the cowboy.

"Can you dig two more?" the cowboy asked Albert. Albert had those holes dug before you could count to twelve.

Albert saved that young cowboy's ranch that day. And, the cowboy wanted him to stay and work on his ranch forevermore, and so he did. Albert saved that ranch many times over after that, and he and the young cowboy became good friends over those many years."

The old cowboy looked at me as if to say, *that's the end of the story.*

"So," asked that old cowpoke, "do you still think that armadillos are not good for anything? Please don't ever say that they aren't, because Old Albert is not with us anymore, and I am that young cowboy from long ago!"

NOW, SLEEP TIGHT, LITTLE PARTNER.

Good night.

SHEA, THE CRICKET WHO CHIRPED, CHIRPED, AND CHIRPED

In a meadow, where everything was green, beautiful, and peaceful, there lived a family of crickets. This meadow had a stream running through it, and the water running over the rocks seemed to be singing a lullaby. It was a truly nice place to live, and those crickets loved the peace and quiet of that meadow.

It *WAS* such a wonderful place to live, until *THAT* day! Ask any cricket which day I am talking about, and they will definitely remember. It was such a different day for them, they will never, ever forget it. You see, this was the day that Shea came to visit their meadow.

Now, Shea was a cricket, just like them... almost. Shea just loved to chirp. She wasn't mean, or cranky. She just loved to chirp, that is to talk in cricket talk. You all know that cricket talk is chirping. And, could Shea CHIRP! She chirped all the time.

Anywhere and everywhere.

Anytime!

151

To anyone and to everyone!

As I said, She just loved to chirp.

All of the other crickets in Cricketville were about to ask her to leave their meadow, so that it would be peaceful and quiet once again, when *it* happened.

All of the younger crickets had left the meadow, to play in the woods nearby. They were having so much fun playing, that they didn't notice how much deeper and deeper into the woods they were getting. When it became time to go home, no one knew which way to go. They were lost in the woods, but good.

The young crickets' parents were beginning to worry, because their children had not come home yet, and it was getting very late. Off into the woods they ran to find their little ones. Finally, they found the children, who by this time were very far into the woods. The cricket kids were scared, but safe. Then, guess what... all the parents discovered that they were lost, too. What were they going to do? None of them knew the way home!

Just then, one of the big crickets heard something. It sounded like a cricket chirping. Listen closely. Do you hear it? In fact, the chirping *was* from another cricket. It was Shea chirping! She was chirping louder than ever before.

The parents just listened to Shea's chirping, and kept

walking towards her chirps.   In no time at all, every parent, and every child cricket was back in that beautiful meadow again, all of them safe and sound.

What a wonderful sound Shea's chirping became for them that day. Not a one of the other crickets ever asked Shea to leave the meadow after that. They all loved Shea for her life-saving chirp, and wanted her to stay with them, forever. After a while, they even asked Shea to never stop chirping, and that made her very happy, because as we all know, she was one cricket who loved to chirp!

Now, close your eyes, and listen... can you hear it? Chirp, chirp...which in cricket language means...

Good night.

CHIP, THE SLOW SLOTH

In a jungle in a place far, far away, there lived a family of sloths. There was the father sloth, and the mother sloth, and their little sonny-boy sloth, Chip.

Their home was in a very nice jungle, as jungles go. It had pretty, tall trees, which seemed to reach up into the sky. It had babbling brooks that made you want to lie down and take a nap, anytime you were near them. You could almost hear the running water saying, *lie down, take a nap... lie down, take a nap*. And many times I did just that!

This jungle also had long vines hanging down from the tree limbs; those vines just seemed to invite little boys to come and swing from them. Wouldn't you like to live in that jungle with Chip and his sloth family? Sounds great!

Most of Chip's uncles and aunts lived on the other side of that same jungle, which was also a nice place to live. Chip loved to visit his relatives and friends on the other side of the jungle. Sometimes he would spend the entire summer over there, at all his cousins' houses.

You may be thinking, *why just the summer?* Well, Chip had to go to school the rest of the year. Did you know that sloths go to school just like you kids do? I actually never knew that either, so why don't we just pretend that Chip does go to school. Can you close your eyes and imagine Chip going to school with a big backpack on his back? Can you just see it?

Now, everything was fine among the sloths on both sides of the jungle, until *THAT CERTAIN DAY!* THAT CERTAIN DAY was a very unusual day for the jungle. You see, it is usually very warm in the jungle, but this day was different. The sloth weatherman, on the sloth T.V. weather show, was telling everyone about *very cold* weather expected in the jungle.

Now, no one in the jungle had even one warm coat. And, no one in the jungle had any warm shoes. In fact, nobody in the jungle had any warm anything. But, Chip's father, as a grownup, knew how to solve problems. He knew how to make a fire, in order to stay warm.

However, the sloths on the other side of the jungle didn't know how to make a fire. Which was probably a good thing, since fires can become dangerous, if you don't know what you are doing. Fire can be used for good things, if a grownup makes it and someone is always around to make sure that everyone is safe, but little sloths should never try to make a fire. *Little kids* should never make a fire, either.

Chip's father made a fire, and he asked the leopard to take some of it to the other side of the jungle for him.   Do you know why Chip's father asked the leopard to take the flame? That's right, the leopard is very fast, and sloths are very, very slow.

The leopard grabbed the flaming candle, and took off running as fast as he could go. But he ran so fast, that the wind blew the candle out. Back to the sloth's home he ran.

Chip's father thought for a minute and said, "I know, I'll ask the jaguar to take the flaming candle to the other side of the jungle for me!"

The jaguar was happy to be able to help. He took that candle and, *whoosh*, he was gone. But he soon came back, and once again, the candle was not burning. It seems that the jaguar was even faster than the leopard, and he didn't get as far as the leopard did, before that candle was blown out.

"What am I going to do?" said the sloth father.

"Let me take it, let me take it," said Chip. "If I run as fast as I possibly can, I still can't move fast enough to blow the candle out."

"But, can you get there before the cold weather sets in," Chip's father asked?

"Sure I can," said Chip. "The cold weather won't be here for four more days, and if I run as fast as I can, I will make it."

So, off Chip went as fast as he could go, carrying that candle with the flame. He ran and ran, and then he ran some more. That candle never even flickered! One day went by, then two. Will Chip make it? Do you think he can? Of course he will make it, because he is the hero of this story. On the third day, Chip was getting very tired, but he wouldn't quit. After all, he just had to help his friends and relatives on the other side of that jungle!

Day four came, and Chip was getting closer and closer. He felt the wind getting colder and colder, but he would soon be there. Finally, he saw the lights from his favorite cousin's house glowing brightly in the distance.

Well, Chip was exhausted from four days of running, but he seemed to run even faster on his way down to that house. Just as he was about to take that final step, he tripped and dropped that candle! This is not a mean story, so the candle did not go out. I tricked you though, didn't I?

Chip picked up the still flaming candle, and gave it to his uncle sloth, and they made a nice fire from it. That fire kept Chip, and all of his relatives, and all his friends warm, the entire time that it was so cold.

Chip saved the day! Chip is the hero. Everyone in the jungle loved him.

Now you can see that you don't have to be the prettiest,

Bob Morgan

or the handsomest, or even the fastest, to be a hero.
In that *s l o w* sloth language,

G   o   o   d   n   i   g   h t   !

**CHIP, THE SLOW SLOTH,
CARRYING THE FLAME TO HIS FAMILY.**

158

A SOFTBALL-LOVING TURTLE NAMED SNAPPER

It was a pretty softball field. It had nice green grass. It had shade trees all around the outside edges. It had lots of space for people to park their cars. It even had wonderful running water, in a nearby stream. That softball field had everything.

Snapper lived in that stream, and he loved to watch the kids playing softball. He always wanted to play softball too, but Snapper is a turtle, and turtles don't play softball, or do they? After all, turtles don't have hands to hold the bat with. They can't run very fast. And they sure can't pitch the ball to the batter. What do you think Snapper could do if he played softball? Let's get on with our story, and maybe we'll find out!

What a beautiful day, Snapper thought, yawning as he woke up that morning.

The sun was shining, and the day was nice and warm. The birds were chirping, and all the squirrels were scampering about in the treetops, as though they were playing tag.

"It would be a good day for me to play softball, if only the kids would ask me," Snapper said, to no one in particular.

Then, as they did every summer day, along came the kids with their softball, their gloves, and their bats. There were lots of kids coming to play today. Many more than Snapper had ever seen before! They formed two teams, and started up their game.

Snapper climbed up onto the bank of the stream to watch, wishing that he was down there playing, too. But, what could he do? Are you ready to find out what a turtle can do in a softball game? It even seems funny to think about, doesn't it?

The first little kid came up to bat. The pitcher hurled the ball to her, and she whacked that softball really hard, but it went the wrong way. That's right! It went straight towards the stream. Even the fastest little kid couldn't catch up to it before, *kerplunk*, it went into the water with a splash.

Now, what will the kids do for a ball? That softball sank right down to the bottom of the stream. And wouldn't you know, it was the only softball those little kids had. What do you think they will do?

Okay, you're right, here's where Snapper can make a lot of friends. He saw that the little kids were upset about losing their softball. He didn't like it when the kids were sad. He just had to do something to help.

What do you think Snapper should do? Did you guess what he did? Where does Snapper live? Can he swim? Can he swim all the way to the bottom of the stream? After all, Snapper is a turtle!

Well, Snapper dove back into the water, and he went straight down to the bottom. He found the softball, grabbed it with his teeth, and swam back up to the top in no time at all. When he came crawling up the stream's bank with that softball in his mouth, all of the little kids started clapping their hands, applauding him. They were so glad to have their ball back, that all of the little kids loved Snapper after that.

Each and every time that ball went into the water, there was Snapper, ready to go get it. He did this for years and years, and he became a very important part of their softball game.

Well, Snapper made new friends every year. He just loved playing with the kids, and those kids just loved having him play with them, too!

Are you thinking that Snapper still wasn't really playing softball? Well, that wasn't the end of our Snapper story.

You see, it goes on and on. Once, the first base pad was torn and gone, and Snapper told the kids that he would be first base. And he was! Every time that a kid would come running towards him, all Snapper had to do was pull his legs and his head inside his shell, and he made a perfect first base. He even played second base once, and third base, too.

Now, do you think that Snapper was really playing softball? All of the kids in the neighborhood sure thought so, and so did Snapper.

Can you close your eyes and see Snapper
bringing the ball up from the bottom of the stream?

Can you hear Snapper
wishing you pleasant dreams, and good night?

Good night.

HOOT OWL AND RONNIE O. POSSUM

Back in the bayou, in a big oak tree with branches that reached way, way out to shake hands with the other oak trees, lived an owl named Hoot. Hoot loved living in that oak tree, and the oak tree loved Hoot living there. They were friends.

Now, under that big oak tree was where Ronnie O. Possum lived. Ronnie O. loved living under that oak tree, because of the wonderful shade it made. In turn, the oak tree loved Ronnie living under him. Why's that, you ask? Well, every time Ronnie moved about, his scratchy little feet would tickle that old tree's roots, and make him laugh.

Hoot would sit on his branch all day, sleeping, and all night looking for food. Did you know that owls can see things which are very far away? Well, they can, and Hoot could see things in the dark that you and I could never see. And Hoot doesn't even wear glasses!

Ronnie O. Possum could not see as well as Hoot. Ronnie really needed to wear glasses, but have you ever seen an opossum wearing glasses? Well, neither have I. Besides, an opossum would look very funny wearing glasses, now wouldn't he?

Since they shared the big oak tree, Hoot and Ronnie would see each other all the time, and say, "Howdy-do?" to each other, but they were never really friends, until *THAT* day! It was the day that those funny looking humans showed up. They had bulldozers, and big machines that were noisy, and woke up everyone in the forest.

"What are they doing here?"
    "What are they doing here?"
        said Hoot and Ronnie at the same time.

It wasn't long before every animal in the forest became noisily aware that those humans were constructing a highway. It was a very big highway. At first, they thought that an empty road would be a nice place to play. The animals could play all of their animal games there, until....

IT happened. Cars! Cars everywhere! That new highway wasn't a safe place to play on anymore. The animals had to move their games way back into the woods, that highway was far too dangerous, now.

But, you know, the highway wasn't really a problem for Hoot. For he could fly anywhere he wanted to go. He could fly over the highway. He could fly over all of the cars, and even the big trucks.

But, it was a really big problem for Ronnie. Ronnie

couldn't fly over the highway. He couldn't see very well, either. Yet Ronnie had to get across the highway, since all of his food was over on the other side. What could Ronnie do?

Well, day after day Ronnie started across the highway, and day after day he was frightened back by cars. Ronnie never did get across to the food.

Ronnie was properly afraid to cross that road, and so he did not eat. Not that first day, nor did he eat the next day, either.

Finally, there came a day when Ronnie was so hungry, he decided he had to do something. He did something that we should *NEVER* try to do! He tried to cross the highway by himself. He took one step out, and a big truck came rolling by, blowing a very loud horn, and almost ran over his toes. He scampered back to the safety of the big oak tree. He was so scared. But he was still so very hungry.

Now, this is the part of the story where we could use us a hero.

Can you think of one?
How about Hoot?

Now, Hoot couldn't possibly fly over the highway carrying Ronnie, could he? No! Ronnie is far too heavy!

Hoot's daytime nap was interrupted by the sound of that truck's very loud horn. I'm sure you know that owls are famous for being able to see very well. But, did you know that they are also famous for being wise? Well, they are…so, with Hoot being so smart, do you think he can come up with some way to help Ronnie? Of course he can, because this is a bedtime story, and bedtime stories always have a happy endings, don't they?

Hoot flew down to the ground and told Ronnie, "Come with me, I will help you cross that highway!"

And he did the very thing that we all should do. He was a grownup, and he was very wise, and he knew that Ronnie should never try to cross that highway by himself. I never cross a street or highway by myself, and you be sure that you have a grownup with you if you ever have to cross one.

Will you make that promise to Hoot and me?

Hoot took Ronnie's hand, and said to him, "I am an owl and I can see very far away. I will tell you when it is safe to cross the highway!" Hoot waited until he could see that there were no cars anywhere, and quickly led Ronnie to the other side.

"Oh thank you," Ronnie said. "But, how will I get back home after I have finished eating?"

"Don't you worry, you are my friend now, and I will come to help you get back safely whenever you are ready. Just call out for me," hooted Hoot.

From that day on, Hoot and Ronnie helped each other every day for the rest of their lives, and they became the best of friends.

So, if you are ever traveling down a busy highway, and you see an owl holding a possum's hand while waiting to cross the road, slow down and let them cross. Who knows, it might be Hoot and Ronnie.

Good night. Be safe.

**HOOT OWL HELPING RONNIE O. POSSUM
TO CROSS THE BUSY HIGHWAY**

Bob Morgan

GERT THE GOOD GATOR

Way, way down in the southern part of this country, down Georgia / Florida way, there live some reptiles we call alligators. We think they are all mean. And all nasty. And we think that we should stay away from them as much as possible. Yes sir, these are some mean and nasty critters, but you know what? They want to stay away from us as much as possible, too. And we should try and stay away from them!

But, this is a story about one of those alligators who wasn't mean, nor was she nasty, and she liked people. That's right! She liked people! This gator's name was Gert. Now, with a name like that, Gert the Gator, she couldn't be too bad, could she? Truly, she was actually known as Gert, the *good* Gator.

Gert lived near a golf course. Do you like to play golf? Does your dad or mom like to play golf? There was a swampy pond near that golf course and Gert just loved it. The water was always clean, in a yucky-mucky way. There was always lots of food to eat, and Gert loved to watch the people playing golf. She would lay in the water with just her two golf-ball sized eyeballs above the surface, and watch, and watch the people play golf.

168

But, the people didn't like Gert! They were always trying to catch her, and trying to move her away from the pond that she so loved. Gert always managed to get away from the traps that those people set out for her. She didn't understand why the people didn't like her. Was it because she was green, and slimy? Maybe it was because she just looked mean. Maybe it was because the people just didn't understand that she was a good gator?

One day as Gert was watching people from far away, playing their game, she saw that one of the men playing golf must be important. She had seen a picture of him before somewhere. He must be very important, since everyone around him was trying to make sure that he was having a good time, and that he was completely safe from harm.

Just then, the very important man hit the little white ball, and it landed right, *kerplunk*, in Gerty's pond, next to her.

"Oh no," he shouted, "My little daughter gave me that golf ball, and I don't want to lose it!"

Which was too bad, because the ball just sank right down to the bottom of the pond. Some of the men with the very important man tried to swim out to the middle of that pond and find the ball, but they couldn't find it.

"I guess that I will just have to tell my little girl that I lost the ball she gave me," the man said.

No one could see that the man had a tear in his eye, no one but Gert!

But what could Gert do to help him? She could easily swim down and find that ball for the man, but she could not give it to him without scaring all those people. What would she do? She wanted to help him so badly! He seemed like such a nice man, caring about his daughter's feelings the way he did.

After the people left the golf course for the day, Gert watched closely to see where the man lived. Why, he lived just across the street.

Gert waited patiently for nightfall. Then, she dove down to the bottom of that pond, and found the ball that the little girl had given to her father. She grabbed it delicately between her jaws, and came up to the surface with the ball in her mouth.

It was very dark now. Night time had finally fallen. Gert waddled slowly to the street, being very quiet, so that no one would see her, or hear her. Looking both ways to be sure there were no cars coming, she crept across the street. She found the man's house, and put the ball on the man's front porch, so he would find it in the morning. Then, Gert went back to her pond to watch as the man came out of his house and found the ball. She wanted to see the smile come back to his face.

Gert had been struggling almost all night long doing this good deed. She was just about to fall asleep as the sun finally came up, and the man walked out onto his porch. She saw him look down, and she saw that big smile all over his face.

Gert felt good! Gert felt so good that she fell right asleep. She was so tired that she fell asleep right out in the open, where all of the people could spot her. She was sleeping so soundly that she never saw that net coming over her.

"At last, we caught her," one of the men said. "We have been trying to catch her for years now. Let's send her to another pond a long way from here!"

This time, it was Gert who had a tear in her eye. For she loved that pond, watching the golfers play, and she didn't want to move away. She was feeling very low.

Just then, the important man came over to see what the fuss was all about. He was holding that ball in his hand.

"Let her go!" he snapped! "Take that net off of her right now and set her free." Of course, the men did what the important man told them to do. They set Gert free.

After all of the people had left the pond, the man looked at Gert and at his precious golf ball.

"This ball was given to me by my little girl, and it is very special to me. I know that you had something to do with getting it back to me, didn't you? Your footprints came up to my yard, and I traced them straight back here to you. I know that you will never understand what I am saying to you, but thank you!"

Gert did understand what he was saying, and thought it was a shame that he would never understand her.

The man told Gert that she could stay in that pond as long as she wished, and that no one would ever try to catch her again.

Gert the good gator lived in that pond for a very long time, and she even got to know that man's name. She thought that it was a very funny name, but she never told him that. After all, he wouldn't understand it even if she did try to tell him, because he couldn't understand alligator talk.

Anyway, that man's funny sounding name was "Mr. President."

Good night.

DOBIE, GABBY, AND THE DEEP BLUE SEA

All you could hear that day was the roar of the ocean, as it came in to meet the shore. It seemed to be wanting to shake hands with the palm trees, and the sea oats that lived there. They seemed to be standing guard over the ocean, not letting anything bother the water as it rushed up to meet the sand.

And then, a loud noise came from the seaside. It was a seagull that had been standing there, listening to the calming sounds of the ocean. He carried his food for the day in a big bag, which he had set down on top of a large sand dune. The wind had picked up his food bag, and blown it into the ocean.

Have you ever been to the ocean? I'll bet you have! Then you know that the wind is always blowing very hard there, don't you?

This seagull's name was Gabby. Gabby didn't know what he was going to do about getting his bag of food back. You see, it was a very big bag, and he couldn't carry it all by himself.

Will he ever get his food back? This is a bedtime story, and bedtime stories must have a happy ending. Or must they? Do you want this story to have a happy ending? Okay then, it will.

Gabby's friend Dobie was an old pelican, who had lived near the ocean all of his life. He had seen many strange things happen in his life, but this was one of the strangest. He chuckled each time he watched Gabby dive for that big bag, and try to grab it with his mouth. Gabby's only problem was that his mouth was just a small, seagull beak... far too small to pick up that bag.

But old Dobie had a big mouth. Have you ever seen a pelican? Do you like pelicans? They do have big mouths, don't they? Old Dobie watched Gabby trying to get his food for a long time, and then decided to go over to help.

"Gabby, would you like for me to go get that big old bag for you" Dobie asked?

"Oh, would you, please," Gabby cried, "I will never be able to carry it, and I am getting really hungry."

So off Dobie went, flying way up into the air. Then he dove straight down towards the bag, and he caught it on his first try. Pelicans are really good at that. He opened that big old scoop of a mouth of his, and the bag just fell in. Old Dobie still had room in his mouth for two more bags that size. What a big mouth!

Then he carried that bag back to the seashore where gabby was waiting.

"Oh thank you, Dobie," Gabby shouted, "If there is ever anything that I can do for you, just let me know and I would be happy to return the favor that you just did for me."

"You are welcome Gabby, for I am your friend, and I was really happy that I could help you," Dobie replied.

Dobie went home that night, feeling very good about being able to help his old friend. But he did think to himself, *how could Gabby ever be able to help me with that small mouth that he has? But, it was very nice of him to offer to help me one day.*

As the years went by, Dobie never did have to help Gabby again. And Gabby learned that he must never try to carry such a big bag in such a little beak.

Gabby did return the favor, but that's another story.

Dobie and Gabby told me that it's time to say...

Good night.

DOBIE PELICAN AND GABBY THE SEAGULL

CLEM CLAM

On the bottom of the ocean floor, and on the ocean's edge, there live many sea creatures. Some are very large, and some are very small.

Can you think of a creature that lives in the ocean that is very big? How about a whale? Is a whale very big? Have you ever seen a whale? Tomorrow, after you wake up, will you look in one of your books for a picture of a whale? Promise? OK!

This story is not about a whale. It is a story about a sea creature that is much, much smaller than a whale. It is a story about a clam. Do you know what a clam is? Tomorrow, while you are looking for a picture of a whale in one of your books, look for a clam, too.

But, let's begin our story before you fall asleep.

Clem Clam lives in two places. He has a home on the ocean floor, and then sometimes he makes a home on the beach, in the mud. Yes, that's right, in the mud. He loves it down in the mud, because no other animal can find him. Also, it is nice and warm down there in the mud.

One day, as Clem was stepping out of his mud home to stretch his legs, and to get some fresh air, he heard a strange noise coming from some nearby seaweed. He found a little sea turtle who was crying.

"What is the matter?" Clem asked the little sea turtle.

"I am just a little turtle, and I have lost my turtle shell, and now I am scared that some bird or animal will eat me," cried the little turtle. "I have lost my shell, and I don't know where I put it! I am very frightened!"

Clem thought for a moment, then said to the turtle, "Don't worry, I will help you find your shell. Turtles move very slowly, so it can't be very far from here."

Together, they looked and looked for that turtle shell, but it was nowhere to be found! What will they do? They had better do something very quickly, because Mr. Seagull was flying overhead looking for a meal to eat, a meal very much like that little turtle.

Clem saw Mr. Seagull, and said to the little turtle, "Quick, come on into my shell with me before that seagull sees you!" Clem opened up his shell as far as he could, and there was just enough room for him and that little turtle.

Well, our Clem saved the little turtle's life that day. And for a long time after that day, every time the little turtle was in danger, there was Clem with his shell open, making a safe home for himself, and for the little turtle.

This is not the end of this story... Before long, the little turtle had grown into a big turtle, and had grown a brand new shell of his own. And in that new shell, he even saved enough room for his old friend, Clem.

Clem just loved to visit the big sea turtle in his shell. And the big sea turtle took Clem on long trips, and for fun rides up and down the coastline, and from the top of the sea all the way down to the bottom of the sea. They certainly had the makings of being good friends for a lifetime.

Clem had no way of knowing that the day he decided to help that little sea turtle would turn out to be the best day of his life.

The big sea turtle just carried Clem back to his home in the mud, so he could go to sleep for the night. And, you know, Clem and the big old sea turtle just told me to tell you...

Good night and sleep tight.

SCOOTER, THE LITTLE ALLEY CAT

Scooter lives in an alley, in a small city, near to where we all live. Scooter is a very nice cat, with lots of other cat friends, though some of them are not so nice! Would you care to hear the story of Scooter, or would you prefer to hear the story of those other, mean cats? Okay, I thought so. Well then, let me begin our story about Scooter, the little alley cat.

Little Scooter loved birds and mice. I don't mean that he loved to eat those birds and mice, I mean that he liked to have them as friends. Most cats like to have birds and mice over for dinner, as their dinner. But not Scooter! Scooter made friends with all of the other animals. He just liked all different types of animals. That's pretty unusual for a cat, isn't it? Well, Scooter is just that - an unusual cat!

You may be wondering by now just what Scooter does like to eat for dinner. Well, he likes broccoli, and potatoes. He also likes spinach and onions. Onions! Nah, I was just kidding about the onions. But Scooter really does like milk. And his most favorite food of all is cat food.

One day, just as Scooter had gotten out of bed to start doing whatever it is that cats do, a group of his friends stopped by to ask him to play with them. He wanted very much to play with them, so off they all went. They were cat-walking and cat-walking, when the big cat, up in front of Scooter, stopped suddenly and stood very still. He motioned for everyone to be very quiet, and he pointed to the ground not far in front of them. There, where he pointed, was a big flock of birds! And those mean cats were fixing to catch some birds to eat.

Now, Scooter didn't want any of the mean cats to eat his bird friends, but what could he do? He also didn't want any of his cat friends to be mad at him, so he just had to think of something smart, and quickly, too!

The mean cats crept closer and closer to the little birds, and were about to pounce, when they heard a loud "AAAAAAAchooooooo." Scooter had sneezed on purpose, to scare the birds away. And away they did go!

The mean cats could not be mad at Scooter, because they had all sneezed before, and they knew that he couldn't help it. But, we all know that he could have helped it this time, don't we?

Then, a little farther down the road, those mean cats saw a field mouse running about, and playing in the grass. The cats became very quiet again. This time, they were sure to get this field mouse for their lunch! Or were they?

Slowly they crept forward, keeping their eyes on that poor unsuspecting little mouse. Closer and closer they came, and then, just as they were ready to pounce, little Scooter stomped on the tail of the cat that who was right in front of him.

"OOOOOwwwwiiiiieeeee," the mean cat screamed! "Ow! Ow! Ow! That hurt," he cried.

"I am so sorry that I stepped on your tail" Scooter said, as he winked at the little field mouse. The little field mouse saw what Scooter had done, and he winked back before he scurried away to safety.

It was getting dark now, and the cats had to be getting back home for the evening. None of the mean cats realized what Scooter had done that day, so they remained good friends. Scooter went home too, and opened up a can of his favorite food. What was in the can that Scooter opened? Did you say onions?

The years passed, and little Scooter started getting very old. But, over those years he had made a lot of good friends. For you see, soon after he saved those birds, and that little field mouse, Scooter saved many other animal friends, and all of those animals really loved him. As a matter of fact, Scooter saved most of the animals he knew, at one time or another. He is, indeed, a very nice cat!

But, Scooter had a problem. You see, as he got older and older, he no longer had the strength to open the cans of cat food anymore. He didn't even have the strength to go to the store, or to carry home his favorite cat food.

   Now here is where this story really gets unusual. Have you ever seen a bird open a can of cat food? Have you ever seen a field mouse feeding a cat?

   Just go on over to Scooter's house if you don't believe this story is true, and you will see for yourself that it can happen. Or can it?

   Now, close your eyes and picture a field mouse helping out a little, old cat... keep looking, and...

                        Good night.

TODD FROG
AND HORTENSE HORSE

Todd Frog lived near a big pond, which was right in the middle of a pasture. He loved living in that pond. It was a nice place to go swimming in the summertime. It was also nice in the wintertime, because when the pond was covered with ice, Todd would put on his ice skates and go skating. You must be wondering if frogs really do go ice skating! Most frogs really don't, but Todd Frog does. He is a very special frog.

Hortense Horse lived right in the middle of that same pasture. She loved living in that pasture. Summertime, when all of the grass was at its very greenest, Hortense would eat and eat. She loved the green grass. In the wintertime, the grass would turn to hay, and Hortense loved that, too. And she had the nearby pond to drink water from. Are you thinking that Hortense loved to ice skate, too? Not Hortense! She loved to dance like a ballet dancer.

Even though Todd Frog and Hortense Horse lived close to each other, they never met, until...

Until that fateful day when all of *those flies* came to the pasture. You may be wondering what in the world flies have to do with this story? Do you know what a pest a housefly is? Well, houseflies love to annoy horses, too (then they are called horseflies). Our poor Hortense only had her tail for a flyswatter. Those pesky flies seemed to be everywhere! Poor Hortense, what could she do?

She would shake her head and stomp her feet, trying to chase those flies away. But they came right back.

Todd Frog had seen Hortense Horse many times in the pasture. He knew that she was a nice horse, as horses go, and he wished that he could do something to help her. And, kids, he can do something, can't he?

What is one of a frog's favorite foods? Did you say flies?

Todd Frog hopped all the way over to Hortense Horse to ask her if he could help.

"My name is Todd Frog," he said to Hortense, introducing himself. "Can I be of help?"

"My name is Hortense Horse," said Hortense, "can you save me from these pesky flies?"

Todd said, "Flies are my favorite meal! Be very still, and I will hop up onto your back."

Hortense stood very still and let Todd jump up on her back. It even tickled a little. Todd flicked out his tongue, and caught the first fly. Then another, and another, until bye and bye all of the flies were gone.

Todd and Hortense became really good friends that day,
and all because of those pesky horseflies. Todd never let
any flies bother Hortense ever again.

Then came a day when Hortense had the chance to help
Todd. And, of course, she was happy to help him. It
seems Todd had some friends that he wanted to visit, but
they lived far away in another pond. It would always
take Todd weeks to get there, for he had to hop all the
way. And, of course, he would have to hop all the way
back home after his visit... it was very tiring.

Well, Hortense told Todd, "Hop up on my back and I
will have you there in just a jiffy, I am a racehorse, and I
can run really, really fast!" Todd jumped up, and held
on to Hortense, and away they went, lickity-split!

Todd visited his friends all day, and he still made it back
home the same day, because of Hortense. That frog and
that horse sure were good friends, weren't they?

So, if you are ever riding by a big pasture, with a big
pond nearby, and see a horse standing around with a frog
on his back, be sure to wave to those two best friends!

Good night.

JACK, A HALLOWEEN PUMPKIN WITH A HAPPY FACE

This story happened a very, very, very long time ago. It was so long ago, that your grandfather wasn't even born yet. It's about a Halloween pumpkin, named Jack.

Now you may think that Jack is a funny name for a pumpkin. So did I! But his middle name is even funnier. It is Oliver. Do you think that is a funny name for a pumpkin? Well, wait until you hear what his last name is. It is Lantern. Those are great names for people, but I don't know how he got those names, him being a pumpkin and all! Do you?

It was getting close to Halloween, and all of the neighborhood kids were scrambling about looking for pumpkins to carve out, so that they could make ugly, spooky faces. They looked, and looked all over the countryside trying to find just the right pumpkin. Finally, they saw a great big pumpkin patch. It had all kinds of pumpkins in it. It had tall ones, it had short ones, it had skinny ones, and it had big old round ones, too.

Jack lived in the back of the pumpkin patch, in a corner where hardly anyone ever saw him. All of the kids picked out their favorite pumpkins in that patch, and pretty soon almost all the pumpkins were gone. All except Jack! Poor Jack sat there and sat there hoping to be picked, but no one had even seen him.

It was getting closer and closer to Halloween, and Jack was still sitting there in that old pumpkin patch. Then he saw a little girl coming towards him.

"Oh, I hope she picks me," Jack cried. And she did!

"Oh, my, what a pretty pumpkin you are," she said. "Just look at that wrinkle that you have on your face. It looks like you are smiling. I want to take you home with me!"

The little girl took Jack home, and sat him on her porch. Then she took Jack's hat off, and placed a small light right in Jack's pumpkin shell. Boy, did he look pretty!

All of the other kids put scary faces on their pumpkins, and they were ugly! When the very little kids came by, they were so frightened that they wanted to run home.

And then the little kids saw Jack with that pretty smile on his face. They weren't frightened of Jack. They even wanted to pet him, and to talk to him. Pretty soon all of the neighborhood kids had heard about Jack. And most of them came to see him. Jack was so proud!

Now, you might be wondering why I took all the time at the beginning of this story to tell you about Jack's name.

Well, think about it for a few seconds... every year at Halloween, you hear and say his name many, many times over!

Why, that's right, it is.... Jack O. Lantern!

Good night.

JACK O. LANTERN, THE SMILING PUMPKIN

SUE AND TAMMY
AND THE MAGIC WISHBONE

Sue and Tammy were sisters who lived in a small city. The same city where you and I live. They lived in a tiny, but very nice house; but, they were never happy with the house, because most of their friends had much bigger houses, and they wanted to live in a bigger house, too. But all that was about to change.

It was getting close to Thanksgiving, and all of the houses on Sue and Tammy's street were decorated for the holiday. Some of the houses had bales of hay in their yards, with pumpkins on top. Some houses had scarecrows, and some had long stalks of corn, all stacked up as their decorations. The whole neighborhood looked very much like Thanksgiving.

But not Sue and Tammy's house. They just couldn't get themselves into the mood for Thanksgiving.

"What do we have to be thankful for," they asked each other? You know, *THEY WILL SOON FIND OUT.*

The day finally came for the big Thanksgiving dinner. It was getting very cold outside. Sue and Tammy looked out of their window, and they saw an old man who had no place to sleep, or a place to get into, out of the cold. But the old man soon walked away. Sue and Tammy forgot all about that old man, as soon as they once again saw those big houses across the street. They wanted to live in a big house so badly.

That evening, Tammy and Sue's father started carving the turkey. He was such a good father, he always had a twinkle in his eye. Their mother began setting the table, making room for all of the good food that they had to eat. Their mother always had a smile on her face, too.

When they were about halfway through eating that wonderful meal, Sue said "Look, I have the wishbone, let's make a wish."

So, Tammy and Sue both held the wishbone in their hands, in order to make a wish. And do you know what happened next? Everything around them just seemed to stop. Their father and mother didn't move. The fire in the fireplace just stopped burning. Everything, time and place, just seemed to stop.

Then the wishbone spoke... "I will give you two wishes, but be sure they are wishes that you really want, because you will never have another one from me."

Tammy and Sue smiled at each other without saying a word, because they already knew what they wanted for their first wish. That big house! They held on to that wishbone, and made their wish.

POOF!

All of a sudden, their house turned into a great big, beautiful home. It was all they had ever wanted, or was it?

They looked up from the table, and where were their parents? They were gone!

"What did you do with our mommy and daddy," asked Sue and Tammy?

"You only wished for a big house," said the wishbone. "You didn't wish for your parents to stay."

"Why is it so cold in here," asked Sue?

"Well, you didn't ask me to make the house warm," said the wishbone.

"Where is all our Thanksgiving dinner," asked Tammy?

"You never asked me to keep the Thanksgiving dinner," answered the wishbone.

"What happened to all of the toys that our father and mother gave us," both Sue and Tammy asked at the same time?

"You did not ask me to keep your toys, either. All you ever asked me for was this big house," the wishbone said.

Suddenly, it became clear to Sue and Tammy that they

already had everything important to have, when they had their little nice house.

They had the crackle of the fireplace, and their parent's love to keep them warm.

They had all of the toys of a lifetime, which their parents had given to them with love in their hearts.

They had all of the food that they could want to eat, because their father and mother worked so hard to make sure that they were never hungry.

They missed the twinkle in their father's eye. They missed their mother's gentle way of showing them that she loved them.

They were really scared, and started crying. "What have we done?" mommy

Then, the wishbone said to them, "Don't forget that I gave you two wishes, but be very careful what you wish for this time, it's your last wish."

Both Sue and Tammy knew what to use that last wish for!

"Wishbone, let us have our lives back the way they were before we made that first wish."

"Are you sure? For I can never come this way again."

"Oh yes, we are sure," the girls said.

POOF!

The girls opened their eyes, and saw father with his twinkle, and mother with her kind, gentle ways. It was as if nothing had happened! Everything was the same as before, and the girls were so very happy about that.

"Father, mother, where were you a little while ago?" "Where did you go?"

"Why, we have been right here," said the father.

"We never left the table," said mother. "We've been sitting right here, the whole time you two girls were sleeping."

"Sleeping," Sue and Tammy asked each other? "Were we just dreaming all of that?"

The two girls went outside right away, and found the old man they had seen before. They brought him in out of the cold, and they gave him some of their wonderful Thanksgiving dinner.

Then they found some cornstalks, and decorated their small, beautiful home for Thanksgiving.

Now they understood what was truly important in their lives, and it certainly wasn't a big house... this year, they knew what to be thankful for.

The girls went to sleep that night, not really believing that it was a dream about the wishbone. It all felt too real.

So, the next time you pull on a wishbone, be sure to look at what you already have, and be very careful of what you might wish for!

HAPPY THANKSGIVING, and good night.

SUE AND TAMMY MAKING THEIR WISH

FRANKIE FROG
AND THE CHRISTMAS TREE

Frankie was one sad little toad frog. He was sad because
none of the other frogs would play with him. All of
Frankie's so-called friends were green tree frogs. They
played all day in the trees, tossing nuts and berries to
each other, and never tossing one to Frankie.

I wish they would let me play too, he thought. *That looks
like so much fun! They are always laughing and I am
always sad.* Frankie thought to himself... *I'll bet they will
let me play when we get older.*

Day after day passed, then month after month, and
those little green tree frogs never asked him to come play
with them. Poor sad, little Frankie.

Well, the days started getting colder and colder. Winter
was here, and that meant that Christmas was almost
here, too.

Frankie looked down into the nearby city and saw
beautiful lights, and heard Christmas carolers singing
soft, wonderful songs.

He saw people all over the city smiling and being friendly to each other. All of the people were smiling, except for one little girl. Her dress and her coat were torn, and her shoes were so worn out that you could almost see through them.

"I think I will go down there and see if I can make her smile," said Frankie, as he started down the slippery hillside.

The snow and ice were really hard to stand up on, and guess what happened to Frankie. On the way down the hill, Frankie slipped on some ice, and he started to roll. He rolled, and rolled, and he hit a big rock, bounced off of it, and landed right, smack in an open bucket of red paint.

"Boy, I am glad that I am alright, and that nothing is broken," Frankie said, as he climbed out of the red mess.

So he kept hopping on down that hill, being just a little more careful this time. He wanted to see that little girl, the one with no smile on her face.

The little girl went into her house before Frankie could catch up to her. Now, the house was very small, with cracks in the walls. Why, you could even see right through it in some places.

Peeking in, Frankie saw the Christmas tree. There were no decorations on it. Frankie didn't know it, but there were no decorations on it last year, either.

Frankie slipped carefully through a crack in the wall, so he could get out of the cold, and stay warm for the night.

When he got inside, it was so warm that Frankie wondered, *how can that little fire in that little fireplace keep it so warm in here?*

Then he saw the mother, and father, and their little girl all holding hands. *Why, it's their love that keeps this house so warm.* Frankie wished that someone would love him that much.

Do you think that anyone will ever love Frankie? Do you think that anyone would ever love a toad frog? You know, I believe that someone just might!

The mother, father, and little girl went to bed after their goodnight kisses. Their love for each other sure did keep the house nice and warm.

So, our Frankie hopped closer to the fire to stay warm for the night. He passed by a mirror, and he saw a red toad frog looking back at him.

"Oh, no, what am I going to do now," he cried. "Surely, no one will ever play with me now, because I look funnier than I did before!"

Suddenly, an ember from the fireplace shot out, landing right on Frankie's toe.

"Ow!,Ow!" he screamed, as he jumped straight into the

Christmas tree. He was jumping so hard, and so fast, that he put red paint all over that tree, and turned it into the most beautiful Christmas tree you have ever seen!

Well, by-and-by, the pain in Frankie's toe finally stopped, but he was feeling very tired, so he decided to just go ahead and sleep on the prettiest branch of that tree.

The next morning, the little girl came out and saw the tree.

"Mommy, daddy, come look at the Christmas tree. It's the most precious tree I have ever seen."

Then she saw Frankie asleep on that wonderful branch. "I'll bet that you had something to do with this tree, didn't you? Won't you be my friend?" she asked softly, as she gently woke him.

As Frankie came awake, he saw the little girl looking at him, and what did she have on, but this beautiful, beaming smile.

So, from then on, Frankie and the little girl always had smiles on their faces. And Frankie couldn't wait until next Christmas, because he already knew how to decorate a Christmas tree!

Good night, and a very
MERRY CHRISTMAS
FROM MY FAMILY TO YOURS, BOB.

A CITY FULL OF SAD PEOPLE

This is a story about a city that had no happy people. It was a very sad city. No one walked around with a smile on their face. No one petted the cute puppy who lived on the corner. No one spoke softly to the little kittens playing in the cardboard box beside their mother cat. Oh, I tell you, this was a very unhappy city. It had always been that way in this city. But, that was about to change, forever!

Little Molly came to that city one bleak and cold winter day. Molly was an orphan, who had never known her parents. She never had pretty clothes to wear, and she never had warm shoes for those cold times. But Molly had something that no one else in the sad city had. It was all that she had, but she gave it away freely. It was a smile!

You know that when someone smiles at you, you just have to smile right back. The first person Little Molly met when she came to sad city was the grocery store owner. When she walked up to him and asked what the price was for an apple, the grocer saw that she didn't have enough money to pay for it. But, *she smiled*, and started to walk away.

200

"Wait a minute," the grocer shouted, "I think you do have enough money for this apple!" And as he handed Little Molly that apple, he wondered why he did that? He didn't know it, but Molly's smile made him feel different! Why, he almost smiled back!

Then, Little Molly went to the restaurant to try to find something to eat. The man in the restaurant asked her what she wanted, and she said that she hadn't eaten all day, except for an apple. The man said that the food in his restaurant would cost a lot of money, and Little Molly saw that she didn't have enough to pay, so *she smiled* and turned around to leave.

The man cried, "Wait. If you would clean the tables afterward, I'll give you all the supper you can eat tonight!" *Why did I say that?* the man thought.

It was that smile!

After she had eaten and gotten her tummy full, and cleaned the tables, Little Molly went to the hotel to see if she could find a place to sleep for the night.

The hotel clerk said to Molly, "The rooms cost a lot of money, do you have enough?"

"No," said Little Molly. Then *she smiled,* and turned to walk back outside, into the cold, dark night.

"You know, I do have one room that you can use tonight, if you will make up the bed tomorrow!" That old hotel clerk didn't know what made him say that! Perhaps it was Molly's smile?

Little Molly woke up the next day with her tummy still full, after a long night's rest, and she felt really good. It made her smile even more precious. Then, she continued on her way!

That same morning, the grocer met the man from the restaurant on the street, and they gave each other a big smile. *What is happening to us*, they thought. Whatever it was, they sure liked it because it made them feel much better. Then they both met the hotel clerk on his way to work. All three of them smiled at each other, and each one of them felt much better.

"Why are we smiling?" they asked each other. "It must be that little girl named Molly who was here yesterday. She has made us all smile. And we like it!"

Pretty soon the whole town was smiling. It is now a much better city than it was before, and all because of Little Molly and *her smile*.

It was getting close to Christmas now, and all of the people in sad city wanted to find Little Molly, and to help her, because she had given them something special that money could not buy. They wanted to give her presents, a new pair of shoes, a new coat, and a home to live in.

But Little Molly could not be found. She seemed to have disappeared. Now the residents of sad city decided to change the name of their home town to Mollyville. And oh, she would have liked that.

Christmas was now only days away, and still no Molly. Finally, the day came, Christmas Eve. All of the people in Mollyville were becoming sad again, because they could not find Molly anywhere. They couldn't eat, they couldn't sleep, and they did not know what they were going to do without little Molly.

So, they all gathered together to do something they had never done before. They all started singing Christmas carols. And while they were singing, each of them was thinking of Little Molly, and of *her smile*. What a difference one little girl's smile had made.

Then they heard it! The sound of reindeer on the rooftops. That jolly old "HO", "HO", HO".

They couldn't believe it. They had stayed up so late worrying about Little Molly, that they actually caught Santa bringing gifts to all of the boys and girls in Mollyville.

The kids got more gifts than ever before, because they were all smiling and friendly now, and, you know Santa loved that! And so did that little girl, riding in Santa's sleigh. She was helping Santa, and smiling so beautifully, as she tossed those gifts right down the chimneys!

MERRY CHRISTMAS TO ALL!!

...and to all a good night!

Bob Morgan

ABOUT THE AUTHOR

Robert A. "Bob" Morgan was born in Federal Point, Florida, a small community located on the Saint Johns River, between Palatka and Hastings. His family moved to Hastings, a farming town, when he was only a few years old, and Bob spent all his school years there, graduating from the Hastings High School in 1961. Bob Morgan is proud to say that he still has numerous friends in the Hastings area.

Bob entered the world of agriculture soon after graduating from high school, and has been involved with farming interests in both Florida and Ohio. He enjoyed the world of agriculture for some forty years.

Mr. Morgan was never without companionship, coming from a family of eighteen siblings, most of whom remained in Florida, with a few spreading out into Georgia, Virginia, and California. Bob remains very close to all of his brothers and sisters. Mr. Morgan is married, with wonderful children and grandchildren. His family remains the light of his life.

When his own sons were very young, they would ask him to read them bedtime stories; Bob would ask them to name a subject. He would then proceed to make up personalized stories for them, based on their selected subject...how his own kids loved those stories. Over the years, Bob's wife, Sam, would ask "why don't you write some of those stories down?"

Well, lucky for us all, when Sam talks, Bob listens. Bob's children's bedtime stories are featured weekly in four local newspapers, where they are immensely popular. It seems that advertising revenues have increased due to Bob's weekly columns, with local businessmen competing to have their ads appear on the same page as the bedtime stories. Bob's homespun style has folks thinking of him as the modern-day Uncle Remus. An effort is now underway to syndicate these remarkable stories into newspapers throughout the United States and Canada.

This wonderful book, *Bob-Tales*, is the first of what we trust will be a series of Bob Morgan's children's bedtime stories.

Bob Morgan hopes that you will enjoy reading these first fifty tales, and that your children and grandkids will enjoy hearing them.

Amy Renee Banton

Cover artist and illustrator, Amy Renee Banton, is originally from Boca Raton, Florida. She relocated to St. Augustine to study fine arts at Flagler College.

She is currently a visual arts teacher at a local middle school, and is also an accomplished freelance artist. Mrs. Banton excels with her oil paintings of St. Augustine history, and many of her pieces are currently on display in local galleries.

She currently resides in St. Augustine, Florida with her husband Ted and beautiful daughter, Marley.

LaVergne, TN USA
20 July 2010
190147LV00001B/230/A